"Beck!" Katelyn's voice broke through the chaos in his mind.

Panting for breath, he dropped the ax at his feet on the top step along with pieces of wood.

"The door is dead," she said. "No need to keep hacking."

He stared through the exit he'd opened up in the door at the glowing landing. "I'm not sure we can get out this way."

There were no good options.

"Help! Can someone hear me? Help us!" Katelyn had left his side and gone back to the windows. She shouted through the opening that was much too small to escape through.

But how could anyone help them, even if they heard her cries? Beck was done deliberating about what to do next. It was time for action.

"We have to face the flames, Katelyn. It's the only way. I'll go up and check it out first."

Katelyn grabbed his arm. "No. You can't."

"Neither can I let you die here."

Elizabeth Goddard is the award-winning author of more than thirty novels and novellas. A 2011 Carol Award winner, she was a double finalist in the 2016 Daphne du Maurier Award for Excellence in Mystery/Suspense, and a 2016 Carol Award finalist. Elizabeth graduated with a computer science degree and worked in high-level software sales before retiring to write full-time.

Visit the Author Profile page at Harlequin.com for more titles.

COVERT COVER-UP

ELIZABETH GODDARD

LOVE INSPIRED SUSPENSE
INSPIRATIONAL ROMANCE

LOVE INSPIRED® SUSPENSE

INSPIRATIONAL ROMANCE

ISBN-13: 978-1-335-72192-1

Recycling programs
for this product may
not exist in your area.

Covert Cover-Up

This edition published by arrangement with Harlequin Books S.A.

For questions and comments about the quality of this book, please contact us
at CustomerService@Harlequin.com.

Love Inspired
22 Adelaide St. West, 40th Floor
Toronto, Ontario M5H 4E3, Canada
www.Harlequin.com

Printed in U.S.A.

When thou passest through the waters, I will be with thee; and through the rivers, they shall not overflow thee: when thou walkest through the fire, thou shalt not be burned; neither shall the flame kindle upon thee.
–Isaiah 43:2

To my only daughter, Rachel. God is always with you.

Acknowledgments

Thank you to all my writing friends and family
who encourage and tolerate me
along this amazing publishing journey!

ONE

Katelyn Bradley stood at the curb and stared at the dark home. No lights were on. Not even a porch light. No surprise since it was after midnight.

Here goes nothing.

The streetlights were few and far between in the neighborhood and shed little light. No dogs barked that might alert her to danger, but she would stay cautious. Shoving aside her fears, she crept forward while remaining aware of her surroundings. She swatted a mosquito that buzzed her ear.

Everything was probably all right.

Bushes edged the porch and the windows around the house. She hoped no one was hiding in the foliage as she continued up the steps and onto the porch. She peered into the shadows around her, but couldn't see a thing. Katelyn knocked on the door, then turned her back to the house and looked around the yard, also glancing at the neighbors on each side and the houses across the street. In her peripheral vision she could see that next door, Clara remained on her own porch watching Katelyn's every move.

After she got no response, she turned to the door again. "Beck, it's Katelyn. Your neighbor. Clara told me she was concerned. She sent me to check on you."

A few more moments passed.

This time of night, he was probably in a deep sleep. He might be furious at her for waking up his son, too. Regardless, she wished he would turn on the porch light and chase away the shadows. She wished he would answer and let her know that he and Oliver were okay.

Clara had informed Katelyn that she'd seen someone creeping around the house. She was a caring elderly woman whom some considered too nosy. Katelyn thought of Clara in different terms—the woman was simply concerned. More neighborhoods needed watchdogs like Clara.

While she waited, Katelyn palmed the gun she kept hidden and tried to decide her next step. Was this another one of Clara's false alarms? Clara had called the police on too many occasions.

Katelyn had moved into the house next to Clara six months ago. Since Katelyn ran a private investigations and security partnership with her brother Ryan's fiancée, Tori Peterson, Clara had turned to asking Katelyn to check on neighborhood anomalies when they occurred, instead of phoning the police.

After too many times knocking and ringing the doorbell, concern tightened her chest. Though she again palmed her weapon, she reminded herself that she was no longer a police officer. The last thing she wanted to do was unnecessarily frighten Beck or his young son, Oliver.

The distinct sound of shattering glass erupted inside the home.

Katelyn tensed. Clara had been right. Unless, of course, it was only Beck knocking over a lamp as he walked in a groggy state to respond to her untimely knocking. But her instincts told her Beck was in trouble.

"Who's in there? Open up!" She paused. "Clara?" she called over her shoulder.

"Yes, dear. I'm watching from my porch."

"Call the police." In the town and county seat of Rainey, the Maynor County Sheriff's Department served that role.

"Are you sure?"

"Tell them Katelyn Bradley requested help."

Still, the police wouldn't get to the home in time and Beck had a child—Katelyn couldn't wait. The struggle inside continued. She tried the doorknob and it turned, which both surprised and relieved her. Holding her weapon at the ready, she entered the home as if she was in her old job as a cop.

She wanted to shout "Police!"

That could stop whatever chaos reigned inside, but then she would be impersonating a cop.

Even now, she wondered who she thought she was, going in to save the day when she'd failed so spectacularly before.

Katelyn focused her thoughts on the moment. Grunts and groans came from somewhere in the home. Clinking and clattering, too. Her eyes adjusted to what little light filtered through the mini blinds from outside. Following the sounds, she rushed into the large comfortable living room, then down a long hallway decorated with framed family photographs and a child's artwork. All this she took in as she prepared for what she might encounter.

"Beck? Are you okay?"

Sirens rang out in the distance. Still, much too far away. Every second counted. Katelyn would continue to search until she found him. She prayed he would be safe, but her gut clenched as dread took hold.

Entering a spacious library, more light spilled in from a neighbor's security light. She spotted an overturned chair and froze. Shards of colored glass from a Tiffany lamp were spread across the wood floor.

And a body… Beck was on the floor.

At the sight, her heart stuttered. Gasping, she rushed forward. "Beck!"

He groaned.

Before she could drop to her knees next to him, a bulky form grabbed her from behind. Katelyn used defensive techniques to free herself, but in the process, the hulking invader disarmed her. Panic engulfed her. He was gaining the upper hand and she had to get back the advantage. Gulping for breath, she knocked the gun from his hand and freed herself, then whirled to face off with the masked man.

When he lunged for her, she kicked him in the throat. As he stumbled back, she tore off his mask. The light spilling into the room lit up his face, and she memorized the details. Katelyn didn't miss the threatening, murderous look in his eyes. Eyes she would never forget.

A display of red and blue lights flashed in the windows and reflected on the walls. Sirens blared.

The now unmasked face scowled. Her attacker swung his massive fist toward her. Katelyn dodged, but he kicked his leg out, too, and she lost her balance, falling to the floor as he fled the room. Katelyn glanced at Beck. Unmoving, he was awake and gave her a pensive gaze as he pushed to sit up.

Deputies rushed into the home. Lights flooded the library.

Guns were aimed at her and Beck as they remained on the floor. Squinting, she held up her identification—her PI credentials. "*I* called *you*."

"I'm the homeowner." Beck shifted to his knees. "The attacker fled the house. Maybe someone should look for him."

Unlike Beck, Katelyn made no movements until the deputies lowered their weapons.

"Katelyn Bradley." Deputy Clemmons, one of her detective brother's friends, helped her to her feet. "What happened here?"

"I walked in on an assailant who had attacked Beck." Katelyn waited for Beck to take the lead.

He held her gaze a moment, then looked at Deputy Clemmons. "I dropped my son off at his grandparents' and when I came home, I walked in on a burglar. He attacked me. Then Katelyn entered just in time." He sent her an odd look.

Clara hadn't mentioned that Beck had just gotten home. She'd only said she'd seen someone creeping around the house. Had that been Beck she'd seen, checking out his home? Not that it mattered at this point.

"Do you need a paramedic? You look kind of beat-up."

Beck's face reddened. He was a fit guy. Worked at some rock-climbing facility. Clara had said he'd once been a world-class rock climber—no doubt he was strong.

"I'm fine." His voice projected confidence. "I was caught off guard."

By someone strong enough to take down Beck Goodwin. Katelyn was glad the law showed up when they had.

Deputy Clemmons started taking their statements and filling out the paperwork for the report stating that Beck had walked in on a burglary and had tried to restrain the thief. Inserting herself into the incident, PI and neighbor Katelyn Bradley had walked into the home and eventually the library, where she found and engaged the assailant, who fled upon the arrival of law enforcement.

"Ah, whose weapon?" Deputy Clemmons asked as he eyed the gun on the floor by a chair.

Now it was Katelyn's turn to be embarrassed. "That's mine."

Clemmons reached down and grabbed it, then handed it over. "Might want to hang on to it." He leaned closer. "I won't tell your brother."

Great. Now he would hold that over her—

he'd wanted a date with her since forever ago. Not happening.

"Well, folks, I think we've seen enough. You startled a burglar. Good thing no one was shot." Clemmons's tone had turned more serious as he held her gaze. He studied Katelyn. "You saw his face."

"Yeah. I got a good look."

"What about you?" Clemmons asked Beck.

"No."

Clemmons acted like he questioned Beck's response, but then focused on Katelyn. "Can you come in tomorrow to look at mug shots? Maybe he has a record."

She nodded. "Of course."

"See you tomorrow then. I'm sure Mr. Goodwin here is grateful to have such a skilled neighbor, but... Katelyn, please wait for us to arrive next time." His last words held a scolding tone.

Of course he would say that. Maybe she deserved that reprimand, but what about Beck's life? Plus, in her mind things weren't adding up. If the attacker had only been a burglar, why had he stayed until the moment the deputies arrived? Why fight Beck and then Katelyn? Why not flee the scene as soon as his presence was discovered in the home?

The deputies cleared out, and Katelyn turned to look at Beck. She should leave, too, but she wanted to make sure he was truly okay. Her heart had beat a little faster the few times she'd interacted with him, which hadn't been many. She lived two houses down from him—on the other side of Clara.

His gray eyes took her in. "I would thank you for barging into my home to play the hero but you could have been hurt. I had it under control. I almost had the burglar."

Seriously? She stifled a laugh. Well, of all the ungrateful attitudes. "You were on the floor when I found you."

"You could have been killed."

A knot grew in her throat. Rather than continue the conversation, she turned and marched home. Two county vehicles were still parked at the curb. One deputy stood at his vehicle and talked on the radio. Were they out looking for the burglar? Or lingering only to make sure he'd fled the neighborhood for good?

Whatever. She didn't have to stick around and listen to Beck's criticism when he should have been thanking her instead. That's what she got for trying to help. The man didn't appreciate it. If she hadn't intervened he could have been killed. He could be dead right now.

She took a shortcut and crossed Clara's lawn rather than using the sidewalk. The woman was nowhere to be seen. Good. Katelyn would be hard-pressed to produce a smile at the moment. Ryan would hear about her involvement tonight sooner or later. Detective Ryan Bradley was her twin, but could be annoyingly overprotective, which was especially true after what he'd been through months ago when he'd almost lost Tori Peterson, the woman of his dreams, now his fiancée. Tori had become Katelyn's partner in her private investigations and security services business—Peterson Bradley Investigations.

Let them find out in good time. She wouldn't bother either of them at this hour. Her brother and Tori were getting married this coming weekend and Katelyn wouldn't throw a wrench into that event, especially since it seemed that some obstacle was always getting in the way. She was happy they had both found each other. She'd thought she'd found love once but had been betrayed. Katelyn wouldn't give away her heart again.

Home and in bed, Katelyn tossed and turned, fearing that she would fall asleep and dream again of her failure to protect her partner when she'd been a cop on the Shasta PD. Then she finally gave in to exhaustion…

This was it. She was going to drown in the lake if she didn't do something. But what could she do? Death loomed large and much too near. Her lungs burned as she gasped for oxygen. For

*air. She had to get to the surface, away from the
darkness. Away from the death.*

She kicked and...

Katelyn flung her arms, her lungs screaming.
She was wide-awake now. This wasn't a dream.
Someone was pressing a pillow over her face.

With both hands, Beck gripped the shoulders
of the big man and yanked him from where
he was hovering over Katelyn and smothering
her with a pillow. Beck had broken the man's
hold. The formidable attacker cursed, and before Beck could tackle him, the man whipped
out a gun and aimed at Beck's head.

Katelyn screamed, "No!"

Beck knocked away the weapon as it fired,
the shot deafening. The attacker kicked him in
the gut. Pain ignited as Beck fell against the
dresser and landed in the corner.

The guy fled the room, just as he'd left the
library earlier that evening.

Beck scrambled up and started after him. He
chased him through the dimly lit home, knocking items from a table as he moved past.

"Wait. Come back. Who are you? What do
you want?" Beck called after him.

In the laundry room, the man escaped out an
open window.

Beck caught himself and bent over his thighs.

What was he thinking? Like he really wanted the man to come back and shoot him in the head. But Beck was desperate for answers.

Still, as desperate as he was, he wouldn't chase the guy down. Not when Katelyn could be injured.

He needed to go back and check on her, but first he peered through the window and watched the man disappear across the back alley and into the shadows. Even if he tried, he would never find him now. If the man had any brains, he would leave the vicinity. Should have already left with the recent police presence in the neighborhood.

Dawn would be breaking soon and there would be more eyes to witness his crimes. Beck shut the window and locked it. Had she left her alarm system disarmed? The window unlocked?

Beck left the laundry room and headed into the kitchen to get back to Katelyn. Before he crossed the space, he spotted her. She stood at the hall entrance, staring at him with wide eyes—those big blue-green eyes that had caught his attention the first time he'd met her.

Katelyn trembled—with rage or fear, he couldn't tell.

Though he'd wanted to chase after the man and get the answers he sought, he'd been right to stay behind.

He closed the distance and reached a hand out to touch her, but held back. "Are you okay?"

"I'm fine." She turned her back to him.

He followed as she marched down the hallway to her bedroom, where she flipped on the lights. She stared at her bed and the pillow her attacker had used.

An ache coursed through Beck. "No, you're not. You're in shock."

"Go after him. Go get him," she shouted, tears in her eyes.

"No." Beck stood his ground. He wanted to take her in his arms, but he instinctively knew that would be a big mistake. He was attracted to this woman without even fully knowing her and should steer clear. "You're not all right."

He owed her. He'd been too harsh on her earlier—she'd probably saved his life. But he wished she hadn't gotten involved. "Sit down and I'll get you some water."

He guided her to a plush chair in the corner of her room. He flipped on the small table-side lamp next to the chair and noticed the Bible was open. Before he got the water, he did another check around the home to make sure their attacker hadn't decided to come back. Beck double-checked that all the doors and windows had been locked. Sure, he should probably wait in case investigators wanted to dust for prints. But while he hoped they would look for evidence, he thought it more important to ensure Katelyn's safety. The man had tried to kill her. Even though he'd worn a mask, Beck was sure it was the same guy. Same big shoulders he'd encountered in his own home. He'd locked horns with him twice in one night.

The house secured, he got the water from the kitchen sink, and when he turned Katelyn was standing in his path again. Only this time she held a gun at her side.

"I want to know what's going on right now. Why were you here and able to…?" She choked on the words.

Beck handed her the glass. She set it on the counter. Fine. He took it and gulped it down, aware of every second her eyes remained on him. Then he finished and set down the glass. Her eyes had never left him.

"I was watching your home tonight," he said.

"Why?"

See, this was why he wished she hadn't tried to save him tonight. "I was afraid he would try to kill you."

TWO

A shiver raced up her spine. Still gripping her pistol, Katelyn rubbed her arms. She'd grabbed the gun before coming into the kitchen in search of Beck. What did she even know about her handsome neighbor? Well, except that his form was toned and fit and he didn't appear to have an ounce of fat on his body. That should be good for rock-climbing. Or was it because he was a climber that he had no fat? What was she even doing thinking about his toned physique?

"I should call the police." Again.

The last thing she wanted was for Tori and Ryan to worry about her as they approached the biggest event of their lives. The most important day of all—their wedding. Could be there was nothing to worry about.

If only.

She'd left her cell back in her room and debated leaving Beck alone in the kitchen while she retrieved it.

Beck paced her kitchen and filled the space with his presence. Edgy like a tiger, he prowled around. Counter. Sink. Refrigerator. Counter. Sink. Refrigerator. She instinctively knew the image of this well-tuned athletic guy with his sun-bleached shaggy hair and broad shoulders pacing, as if anxious to escape, would forever remain in her head.

But she wouldn't let that distract her from getting answers.

"I want to hear the truth from you. Why did you think he would try to kill me?"

He stopped pacing to stare at her. Instead his jaw took up the movement and worked back and forth. "I would think that would be obvious." Beck began his incessant prowling again.

"No, I'm sorry, but it's not obvious. What's obvious is that you know something you're not telling me. You didn't tell Deputy Clemmons everything, either."

Beck stopped again, his eyes shifting to her and settling on her face. The disturbed look in them shook her insides.

"What's obvious is that you pulled his mask off tonight. You saw his face. You're the one who can identify him. I couldn't see him because you were standing in the way. Don't you get that?"

Katelyn couldn't voice her thoughts as she absorbed his words. She waited for more information from him. She also waited for him to avert his gaze before she did. She had to stay strong and not back off. Finally, Beck the tiger went back to his feral movements. Ran both hands through his hair.

"I thought he would try to kill you because you saw him. I couldn't know for sure. Call it paranoia." Beck suddenly stopped in front of her and took a step closer. "But I couldn't take that risk that he would hurt you. So… So I waited in the shadows and watched your house."

That lump in her throat again. She struggled to breathe as the memory of a pillow covering her face flashed through her mind. And now she couldn't breathe again for far different reasons. Katelyn gasped but she could get no air.

"Hey, hey. It's okay. I'm here." Beck's voice was soothing as he led her to a chair at the table. He urged her to sit, and she did. All she cared about was getting air. Calming her heart. Composing herself.

At the table, she gripped the white tiled top. Ran her hands over the cold, smooth surface until her heart rate slowed. That she'd so easily allowed him to guide and comfort her was disturbing.

"I guess I should thank you." She guessed?

Oh, she should definitely thank him, but the way he'd treated her earlier still stung.

He slid into the chair across from her and dipped his chin as if those gray eyes of his could search her deepest thoughts. Her soul. "But you don't want to because of the way I thanked you at my house earlier."

Well. He *had* searched her soul.

When she said nothing, he continued, "I don't blame you."

Beck Goodwin had to be one of the best-looking men she'd ever met. Not that looks should matter too much, but here he was sitting at her kitchen table being all sensitive, too. Her vision blurred. She couldn't afford to get distracted. "You haven't told me what's going on. Who is this person who broke into your home and is clearly much more than a simple burglar, Beck? You owe me the truth."

"I wish I knew what was going on."

"That answer is not going to cut it. You know something you're not telling me. You're hiding something."

"What makes you say that?"

"Just a feeling I got while I was at your house. That so-called burglar was prepared to stay and fight until the police got there. That isn't the reaction of a typical burglar."

He scraped a hand across his scruffy face.

Katelyn wondered what those whiskers would feel like against her cheeks, then quickly banished the thought. She hoped he didn't notice the sudden rush of heat to her cheeks.

"I honestly don't know who he is. But I've been considering hiring a private investigator."

She arched an eyebrow.

"I'm only going to share the *reason* for that consideration with the PI after signing a contract."

"Why not go to the police?"

"With what?" He gave a half smirk. "I don't know anything."

"This conversation seems circular and I'm getting tired. It's late. Or early." She rose. "I'm calling the police to report the incident."

Katelyn was almost surprised that Beck didn't try to stop her.

Fifteen minutes later a county vehicle pulled into her driveway. Deputy Clemmons again.

He eyed Beck and then Katelyn, as if he believed there must be something going on between them. Katelyn explained the events in detail.

"Mr. Goodwin, what *aren't* you telling me?" Clemmons asked.

Beck remained stone-faced and shrugged. "I honestly don't know who the man is or why he was in my home."

"But you decided to watch Katelyn's home in case he came for her because you didn't know anything." Deputy Clemmons let his sarcasm drag out as he scribbled in his tablet.

"And…he wants to hire a private investigator," Katelyn added.

Beck frowned and glanced her way, almost looking a little hurt, as if she'd shared something he'd told her in confidence.

"Is that so?" Clemmons crossed his arms, the tablet dangling from his hand. His gaze slid from Beck to Katelyn. "What time are you coming in to look at those mug shots? I'll put in for a forensic artist if you don't identify anyone. In the meantime, I suspect this will get passed to a detective." He eyed Beck.

Ryan. *No, please.* See what she got for calling the local law? But she couldn't *not* call them.

"Mr. Goodwin, I suspect we'll have more questions for you. Please stay in town." Deputy Clemmons tucked away his pad. "Katelyn, I'm off duty in an hour. I can come sit here at the curb if you want to feel safe."

"Thanks. I can take care of myself." She would get an earful from her brother—she was sure. "Please don't make a big deal about this to Ryan. He's getting married in a few days, and I don't want him worrying about me when he should be focused on that. Understand?"

Clemmons grew taller, as if he was reading some meaning into her request—like his cooperating would get him on her good side. Maybe after this was over, she could have Ryan have a word with Deputy Clemmons. Katelyn wasn't the girl for him.

Or anyone, after Tony's betrayal. Trusting men wasn't on her radar.

Beck had already crossed the sidewalk in front of Clara's home as he made his way back to his house. Deputy Clemmons got in his county vehicle and drove away slowly. She watched Beck disappear as if swallowed up by his house. What had he said to her again? That she'd tried to play the hero?

Well, he'd played the hero and he'd actually been a hero. He'd saved her.

Her record on that score was in the negative. In the red.

As dawn brightened the sky and chased away the bogeymen, Katelyn started down the sidewalk to Beck's house. She glanced over her shoulder and caught the curtains move at Clara's. Did the woman ever sleep? Katelyn reached his porch and prepared to knock. Had it only been a few hours ago when she'd gone into this house and fought with a bad guy? Then had almost been killed in her own home?

The door swung open without her knocking.

Beck left it open and walked away, as if he knew she would come in whether invited or not.

"Okay, I'll do it," she said.

Drinking a glass of orange juice, he stood halfway in the sprawling open concept space that included sofas for the living room, a dining area and an island counter separating the kitchen at the far end. He finally finished. "What are you talking about?"

"You said you were thinking about hiring a private investigator. That's what I do. Or didn't you know?"

"I knew. I wasn't considering you."

Okay. Well, that kind of hurt. But she wouldn't let it show. "And why not?"

He set down the glass on the dining table, and in three quick strides was two short feet in front of her. "You're in danger now. It wouldn't be safe for you."

"You know what I think? I think what would be safe for me is figuring out what is going on. That would be safe. So hire me. I'm going to investigate whether you do or not."

He exhaled, long and hard. "I was afraid you'd say that."

"Well?"

"I don't know." Beck moved back into the kitchen and put some dishes in the dishwasher.

Katelyn followed him. He was trying her patience. "I helped you. Now I'm in danger, so you say."

"I think you experienced the danger up close and personal." He turned to face her. Wary. Untrusting. "Okay, you're on. I'm hiring you only because now we're both in trouble. And I don't think the local law can help us or protect you."

Beck eyed the beautiful private investigator. Her long, wavy brown hair was tangled, not just from sleeping, but also because she'd almost been smothered to death with a pillow. She hadn't once touched her hair or combed her fingers through it, or twisted it behind her head in a ponytail. It was as if she was oblivious to her hair, as well as her beauty. Beck wanted to touch that silky hair—to comb it out and detangle it. To pay it the attention it deserved.

He shook off the thoughts that he shouldn't be having about Katelyn. Or anyone.

God, what if I hadn't watched her house? He remembered the moment he'd seen someone creeping in the shadows. The figure had disappeared around the house. Beck had followed. He discovered the window open. He hadn't actually seen anyone enter, so he took a risk. He couldn't know, but he highly suspected the creeper had become an intruder. So he'd climbed through the window, a creeper himself, but with intent to help and not harm. Then he'd found the man attempting to kill her.

With the morbid thoughts, his hands shook.

Strong and nimble hands that were able to grip stone and hold up his entire body weight as he clung to rocks while hanging hundreds of feet from the ground. But this incident, that this woman was now involved—it had shaken Beck to his core.

He turned so she wouldn't see how unsettled he was and headed into the kitchen. He almost grabbed his empty glass on the dining table on his way but thought better of it. She would more easily see his weakness when the glass shook with his hands.

His life was spiraling out of control.

And had been since the death of his wife, Mia, a year ago. Maybe even before. Why had it taken him so long to find it? He'd made the discovery yesterday and had taken Ollie to stay with his grandparents—Beck's parents—while Beck tried to figure it out. Then when he'd gotten home, he'd been attacked.

Could that be related to his discovery? How was that possible?

He was paranoid. That's what Mia had told him repeatedly…until the day she decided to tell him the truth.

Except he never heard the truth from her.

He sensed Katelyn's warm presence behind him and felt the soft touch to his arm. Electricity surged up and across his shoulders, then blasted through his chest, but he maintained his composure. He squeezed his eyes shut. Couldn't react. Wouldn't let himself feel anything.

He didn't want to hire her, but she was in this whether she wanted to be or not, so she might as well be involved in finding the answers.

"Beck, are you okay?"

He steadied his breathing.

Pictured himself descending a cleft at Castle Crags. It took discipline and control. Mastery of fear and distractions. "Yes. I'm good."

Slowly he turned and avoided looking at her beautiful eyes too closely. "I overheard you talk about your brother. He's in law enforcement?"

"A detective with the sheriff's department."

Not good. More people involved meant more people in danger.

Unless, of course, he was being paranoid. *Please let me be paranoid. Please let that be all it is.*

Except, he knew that wasn't it at all.

"Beck, it's okay. I won't tell him anything you don't want me to. But I won't break any laws, you should know that."

"No one is asking you to." Then it hit him. Suspicions had been gnawing at the back of his mind since he'd been attacked.

He glanced around his home. Grabbed a sheet of paper and pencil, then scribbled on it.

Not safe to talk here.

Her eyes widened, if only a little, but she remained calm. She understood.

He wished he'd realized his home could be bugged—listening devices or cameras, he wasn't sure—before he'd brought her into this. Hired her. But she'd been the one to burst through his front door and face off with his attacker, and had seen the guy's face. He hadn't asked that of her. He should be grateful that she'd been willing to risk her life for him.

"What did you do before?" he asked.

She angled her head. "Before I was a PI?"

He nodded. He was feeling better now, if only putting on a show. Oliver. He had to think about Ollie. He had to resolve this before his son was put in danger, too.

Her face paled. She replied on the page.

I worked in the Shasta PD.

She didn't sound like she wanted to elaborate. Beck opened the fridge. "I should cook us some breakfast."

She pressed her hand over his. Again, that

current between them. She didn't remove her hand and he was powerless to move his. "No," she said.

Katelyn wrote more on the paper.

I'm going home to get ready. I have to look at mug shots. You're welcome to come. We can talk then.

Concern poured from her gaze and reminded him of what he'd been missing this last year, since Mia had been murdered, but he would never allow himself to trust someone again. At least with his heart. Mia's duplicity had destroyed any hope of that. Now big strong Beck found himself crumbling, and everything around him was getting ready to implode.

Paranoia?

No. He could feel the rumble just like he could feel the earth shivering right before an earthquake rocked the ground beneath his feet.

THREE

At home Katelyn set her security alarm, showered and dressed. She stared in the mirror long and hard. Dark circles under her eyes revealed that she'd endured a harrowing night. She needed to conceal them with makeup. Add some blush to her pale skin. Had it only been a few hours since she'd struggled to breathe beneath a pillow? She pressed a hand against her chest, feeling the rise and fall of her breaths there.

Never had she experienced that kind of fear. She blinked away the tears. The memory was so fresh and raw, and she didn't know what she could do to eradicate the images. They might even replace the recurring dreams she had about that moment when she'd failed to take the shot. A kill shot from her could have removed the deadly threat to her partner.

Realizing she'd been holding her breath, Katelyn slowly exhaled. In and out. That's right. She could breathe. There was nothing to fear.

Nothing to worry about. She would work with Beck to eliminate this deadly threat and be done with it.

Except—she squeezed her eyes and gripped the edge of the counter—if she was honest with herself, deep in her bones she admitted she didn't want to be done with Beck when this was over. He'd been a true hero last night. He'd watched out for her when she hadn't known she'd needed protecting. He'd put himself on the line for her. Why?

She had no time to ponder the thousand questions running through her mind about Beck and the mystery surrounding him that had nearly gotten her killed. But she could at least look decent while they solved it together. Though he might hire her as a PI, she instinctively knew he would be right there working alongside her. Beck Goodwin wasn't the kind of man to wait on the sidelines. And, honestly, that was another thing she liked about him.

The only issue she had now was that she absolutely shouldn't be making a list about all things good regarding Beck Goodwin. Katelyn huffed out a breath as if that could end her feral thoughts. She combed out her wet hair and wished she had time to fix it so it looked nice, like Tori's always did. Katelyn had always been no-nonsense.

She set down the comb as she admitted she was only having these thoughts—again—because of Beck. He was, in a word, gorgeous. She had vowed to avoid men, but this particular man had the frustrating effect of making her want to be beautiful enough that he would look at her and think her attractive—and that would be the case even if he hadn't come to her rescue last night.

That was it. She fled the bathroom. Done with primping. Enough was enough.

Someone pounded on the door in a furious manner that told her it could only be her brother. She was glad for the additional distraction and the chance to toss away the foolish thoughts about looking pretty for Beck.

Katelyn opened her door. Ryan's scowl nearly bowled her over. "Katelyn, what's going on? Why didn't you call?"

She dragged him inside. "Shh. The neighbors will hear." She didn't want them hearing Ryan dress her down.

"You mean Clara will hear." Ryan thrust his hands in his pockets and glanced around her home. "But she won't hear because she's busy answering questions about what she saw last night."

"She's the neighborhood watchdog." Katelyn pulled on her shoes and grabbed her bag.

She had plans and they didn't include standing around and listening to Ryan dress her down— in gentle tones, of course. Her hair would have to air-dry.

"Right," he said. "So she might have answers. In the meantime, I'm glad you look like you have some place to go because you need to get out. I'm having your home processed for finger-prints and evidence. Beck Goodwin's home, too. I've already been to his house. The tech team is just pulling up. Clemmons should have secured both homes, er, crime scenes."

Good. Ryan could direct his frustration at the patrol deputy.

"I don't think they're going to find anything. He wore gloves. I remember that much. That and his face. But I was just getting ready to go in and try to identify him by looking at mug shots or talking to a forensic artist if Clemmons got one lined up."

"Good. You go do that while the team takes over. I want this processed correctly."

Bag over her shoulder, she leaned in to kiss her brother on the cheek. "Thanks, Ryan."

Katelyn headed for the door, then paused. *Wait.* She turned around. Ryan was heading deeper into the home.

She rushed after him. "So they put *you* on this?"

He shrugged. "Got a problem with that?"

"Sure I do. One, I'm your sister. You're too close to me to think clearly. Two, you're getting married in mere days." Katelyn seriously didn't want him to worry about her. "And Tori isn't going to be happy with me if I take up your time with something like this. Really, Ryan."

"Really, Katelyn. Get out for a few hours. I doubt it will take longer."

"I'll get out if you promise you won't take this on. That you'll focus on Tori and your upcoming nuptials."

He blew out a breath. "And you know I can't do that until I know you're safe."

"I'm safe. I'm an ex-cop, remember? So I yanked the mask from a burglar's face and got a look at him. He didn't want to be identified. That's all."

"Oh, that's all. So he tries to kill you." Ryan crossed his arms. "Chief didn't put me on this, just so you know. But I wanted to be the one to see you for myself and let you know what's happening."

Relief rushed through her, but it wasn't complete relief. "That's good to know. I want you to focus on what's coming next in your life, Ryan. You've already had to wait far too long for this. I don't want some burglar to mess this up for you. The guy's long gone by now, anyway. I'll be fine. I need to know that you trust me, Ryan. That you're not disa—"

"Stop. I think you're completely capable, sis. I'm proud of you. Just be careful. That's all." Love and concern poured from her twin brother's gaze.

I have Beck to protect me. Phew, she was glad she hadn't said that out loud. She adjusted her purse over her shoulder. "All right. All right. I'm out of here."

Katelyn left her brother to look through her home. Why had her first knee-jerk reaction been that she had Beck to protect her? She didn't need Beck. She had herself. And if that wasn't enough, she had her family. Where would she be if she didn't have the love of her family? Her parents, Ryan, and then her older brother, Reece, and younger brother, Benjamin—Ben.

Outside, she hurried over to her cherry-red Mazda3 sedan so she could back out before the tech vehicles blocked her way. Ryan getting involved and worried about her was exactly what she hoped would not happen.

And just as she climbed in, the passenger-side door opened, and Beck dropped into her vehicle and folded himself into the seat, though she wasn't sure how he managed that feat.

He had a scowl on his face and stared straight ahead, but she had the distinct impression his mind was far from the view through the windshield.

She pulled her gaze from the man before he caught her staring, and smiled to herself. "Okay, then."

"Can we just go now?" he asked.

"You sound cranky." Katelyn started her car. "Don't like strangers looking around in your house?"

He mumbled something under his breath. His muscular form made the inside of her car feel entirely too small, and his woodsy scent wrapped around her. She cracked her window to clear her head.

Another vehicle pulled up to the curb.

"Oh, no," she said. *Oh, no, oh, no, oh, no.*

"What?"

"Tori." Katelyn backed out—she'd leave Ryan to explain everything to Tori. "She's my partner. She works more on the protection side of things, though she helps with investigations, too. We each have our skills, and pick and choose our cases accordingly. She used to be FBI but resigned to work with me, but mostly to stay close to my brother. They're getting married this week. I want this dangerous mystery of yours resolved. Today would be nice."

Beck slid down in the seat almost as if he

didn't want to be seen. She wouldn't tell him his attempt looked comical.

Heading out of the safe and quiet neighborhood—that is, until last night—she drove under the speed limit of fifteen miles per hour and hoped she wouldn't see in her rearview mirror that Tori was following her. On Main Street, she sped up as they headed toward the county offices, where she could look at those mug shots. But she had a feeling she wasn't going to find the perp in those pictures. "Okay, now would be a good time for you to spill."

"No spilling until you sign an official private-investigations document. I want my private business to remain private."

"Seriously? You don't trust me?"

"I trust no one."

"Well, let's swing by my office then, and we'll print those off and the deal will be signed, sealed and delivered. But while we're on the way, there'll never be a better time for you to tell me what you know than when we're alone. We're alone right now. We might never be alone again. Someone might put cameras up and bug everything everywhere we go."

Beck's heavy sigh was becoming a thing.

"I can't tell you," he finally said. "I have to *show* you."

"Well, why don't you show me now?"

"It's back at my house. They told me to leave while they processed the crime scene."

"Uh, Beck…you don't think they'll find whatever it is that you want to show me that is somehow connected to this?"

"No. I don't think they'll find this. I mean, I hope not."

"I guess I should be glad you hired me as your PI."

She felt his eyes on her then, and in her peripheral vision, she caught the heat of his smile. An amazing smile. Her pulse kicked up. Somehow she had to get control over the way Beck sent her heart zinging around inside. Could he see how much he affected her? Oh, she hoped not. In this small space, he could very well hear her pounding heart.

Oh, great, and now her palms grew moist on the steering wheel.

"Watch out!" He reached for the wheel to whip the car around.

But it was too late. Katelyn saw the grille of the truck mere seconds before it slammed into her car. The impact propelled her body forward into an exploding airbag—all of it happening within a millisecond—and her head rocked back against the seat.

And just like that, it happened again…

Katelyn couldn't breathe.

* * *

Pain ignited all over his body and stabbed through his heart.

Beck blinked a few times. His chest throbbed where the seat belt crushed against him, preventing him from flying through the windshield. He struggled to get his bearings. The airbags had deflated, and a smell…

What was that smell? The gas from the bag?

His mind struggled to clear, then finally rays of sun broke through the dark clouds.

Katelyn!

He carefully twisted to look at her. Blood trickled from her temple. He thought his heart would stop. He felt for a pulse and found it. She was only unconscious.

"Katelyn. Please wake up," he croaked.

He had to get her out of here. Metal had crunched together and he couldn't be sure he could actually get out, but he shifted until he could kick and shove the door. With a loud metallic pop, the door clattered to the concrete, dangling by a strip of metal. Gasping for breath, he staggered out and fell to his knees in the street. He drew in a few breaths to keep from losing it. Then he got up and made his way around her crushed cherry-red car. Beck was barely aware of anything going on as he staggered to her side. He only knew that fear had gnawed through his brain and taken over. Fear and urgency.

He glanced around.

The truck. That truck that hit them. He couldn't see it.

No, no, no. This can't be happening again. Not again.

Finally at the driver's side, he tried the door. Her side hadn't taken the impact, for which he was grateful. He wasn't even sure how he'd survived.

"What are you doing? Moving her could hurt her," someone shouted.

Katelyn opened her eyes and groaned. "Beck? What are—"

"Come on, we have to get out of here."

Katelyn shifted until she could pull her legs from beneath the bent steering wheel. Beck assisted her out of the car.

She was alive. He could hardly believe she was alive. Images from long ago flashed in his mind—he'd witnessed the accident, the vehicle that slammed into his wife's car as she was driving to meet him.

And now, he wanted to pull Katelyn to him but he shackled his wants. "Are you okay?"

She blinked up at him. "Did you really just ask me that?"

He glanced around at the cars passing them

that were slowing enough to gawk. A few had stopped to help. "Where is it?"

"Where is what?" she asked.

"Where's the truck that hit us?"

A man stepped forward and reached out. Beck took a protective posture.

"It drove off. I saw the whole thing."

"Did you catch the license plate?" Katelyn asked.

"Sure did."

Sirens filled his ears. An ambulance pulled up next to the car and then two county vehicles arrived. Beck let an EMT look him over.

"I have a bruised chest, that's all." The EMT looked at the car and angled his head at Beck. "You got someone watching over you to survive that."

Beck couldn't respond. His only thought was that his wife hadn't been so fortunate. But maybe Beck had to survive so he could find out the truth about what happened before.

He remained alert and aware of those around Katelyn.

"You should let us take you to the hospital, ma'am. You need the doctor to okay you."

Katelyn looked to Beck as if she somehow understood that his anxiety went beyond this wreck.

He nodded. "You should go. But I'm going with you, as in I'm riding in the ambulance."

The EMT shook his head. "Sir, we don't have room."

"He's going or I'm not going," she insisted. Though she looked like she was in pain, she sent Beck a small smile. "Larry's a friend. He'll let you ride if I say so."

Larry smiled. Brotherly or friendly? Or something more?

Beck appreciated her agreement and insistence that he ride with her the short distance to the local hospital. He couldn't know how determined these people were to kill them, but it appeared the attempts on their lives had escalated. He needed to tell her everything, and soon, so she would have the full understanding of the danger they were in. Except even Beck didn't know all of it. Nor did he know how to truly protect her. He didn't know from what or whom he was protecting her. The sooner they learned the truth, the better.

God, how do I keep her safe? How do I keep Ollie safe? Please show me what to do!

At the hospital, Beck gave Katelyn the required privacy as an emergency-department doctor examined her. Beck paced the hallway outside her room, hoping she didn't have internal injuries. Back at the incident, someone had shouted that he shouldn't have moved her—and they could have been right. But leaving her inside the vehicle if the truck came back to finish the job…

What was wrong with him? He was letting his paranoia get the best of him.

But it wasn't paranoia when those fears turned out to be true, and he would keep reminding himself of that fact.

Half an hour later and Beck was growing concerned. What was taking so long? He moved to knock on the door just as the doctor left the room without a passing glance at Beck.

Katelyn stood in the doorway as the doctor had exited. "It's okay. I'm good to go."

Moving slowly, she pulled him into the room and shut the door.

"Shouldn't you be lying down or something?" he asked. "I'm not sure you're okay, Katelyn. You look kind of pale."

The frown she gave him told him that was the exact wrong thing to say. "I mean, considering you were in a wreck today, you look amazing. But just a little pale, that's all."

"Enough. I don't care how I look. Just now out in the hallway, you seemed worried."

"Yeah. We were just in a wreck. You were hurt."

"Okay, fair point. But I mean, more than

usual. I don't even know you that well and I can tell something more is on your mind. So what is it? What's eating at you?"

"My wife, Mia. She died in a car accident. Only I never believed it was an accident. Someone murdered her." Beck let his eyes say what he wouldn't speak.

Katelyn's eyes held his and he knew she was reading him correctly.

"Wait a minute. Are you saying what I think you're saying?"

"Someone tried to kill us, Katelyn."

"Are you sure this isn't just your unresolved suspicion that you've attached to what happened last night?"

Please believe me. "I'm sure. That was no accident."

FOUR

Katelyn let the words sink in. Horrible, insane words, especially after what she'd gone through.

This couldn't actually be happening. Could it?

Could she believe Beck? Maybe she should have her brother look into Beck Goodwin's background for her, so that she completely understood what she was getting into. *Whom* she was getting into *it* with. For reasons she couldn't explain to herself, much less anyone else, she wanted to trust Beck.

From hard-earned experience, she knew better than to trust *anyone* that much. So why Beck?

As she searched his eyes, he didn't break the connection. Never averted her gaze.

Maybe she had misunderstood. One could hope. "You're serious. This isn't some kind of joke?"

His gaze remained on her as his chest rose with a long inhale, and then it fell. "I wish I was kidding."

Disappointment pinched his brow and he hung his head.

That she'd put the anguish on his face pinged against her heart. "Beck, I'm sorry. I'm just trying to comprehend all of this. I mean, what do the police think? If you're calling what happened to Mia an accident, then it sounds like they believe it was just that."

He moved his hand around the back of his neck. "They didn't buy in to my theory."

Katelyn couldn't take his dejected look. The big hunk of a man seemed to need someone to believe in him. If only he knew she was the last person that could do that. Still, she couldn't help herself and stepped forward. She pressed her hand against his arm, receiving the expected jolt through her core, and urged his hand down. "Beck, I don't know what happened before and I trust that you're going to tell me everything soon, but do you think that maybe an accident is all that happened today? Isn't that possible?"

"It was a hit and run, Katelyn. They fled the scene. There was no reason for their truck to come at us like that." He stared her down—clearly, his earlier hurt was morphing into anger instead.

Better for both of them.

"Were there any witnesses?"

"Yes, the guy back at the scene. He saw everything."

"I was there. You didn't have time to talk to him to find out what he saw."

Beck lifted a business card. "Ray Sanders. He's a plumber. I called him and we talked. He told me everything he told the police, and why shouldn't he? He got the license plate number. We can run that."

"We'll let the police run that and wait to hear what they find out."

He pursed his lips and started pacing the small space. It was a habit she wasn't sure she could get accustomed to—as if she would have need to get used to his habits. She hoped and prayed this investigation wouldn't take long. She had a wedding to attend and then, hopefully, her own life to live. Beck had a life to live, too, with his son, Oliver. She couldn't see a guy like him staying single for long. But until he found closure for his wife's death, he wouldn't move on. At least he could move on, eventually.

Katelyn wished she could move on. Since Tony had utterly betrayed her, she couldn't imagine opening up to anyone, sharing her heart the way she'd always dreamed until the moment she'd seen him with someone else. Even though with everything in her, she wanted what Tori and Ryan had. But that happily-ever-after, marry-the-man-of-your-dreams dream was just that—a dream. Make that a pipe dream.

It wasn't to be.

But Beck, with his determined and passionate eyes, his protective stance, reminded Katelyn of what she would never have. "So how are we going to get out of here since my car is—"

The door swung open and Ryan rushed into the room. Behind Ryan was Tori, her partner.

Ryan and Tori took turns hugging Katelyn. Tori's eyes were slightly red and she smiled with relief, but said nothing as she hugged Katelyn. Ryan's expression, on the other hand, was somber.

Then the expected onslaught of questions ensued.

"What happened?"

"Are you okay?"

"Who was driving?"

"Is your car totaled?"

"Why aren't they keeping you overnight for observation?"

Katelyn didn't for one minute believe that either of them hadn't already gotten the full scoop from Ryan's fellow deputies, but she knew they simply wanted to hear all this from her, and maybe Beck, too.

"The police are searching for the other driver." Ryan's pensive gaze shifted between her and Beck. "What's going on with you two? You were at Beck's home last night when the first break-in happened. Then Beck was in your home to quote 'save you.'" He emphasized the last two words with finger quotes. "Now you're in a car wreck together?"

Heat infused her cheeks because it certainly sounded like "something" was going on. She eyed Beck and knew if she told Ryan and Tori too much, he wouldn't hire her as a private investigator. In any other circumstance, she would try to convince Beck that her brother and business partner could help with the investigation.

But the danger factor was high, and these two deserved their wedding day. Katelyn could handle this on her own.

Now wasn't the time to stand up to Ryan. He knew her too well. So she buried her face in her hands. She'd been in an accident, after all. This was too much to happen in twenty-four hours.

"We can talk more about this later, sis," Ryan whispered, his tone gentle.

As her brother hugged her, she dropped her hands. "It's okay. I'm okay. It was just an accident."

She didn't even look at Beck as she said the words, but still, she somehow wanted to reassure him that she believed in him. She would see this through with him. Katelyn was loyal, if anything, and she wanted Beck to know that. Katelyn wasn't sure why his feelings or his opinion of her were important to her.

Ryan's gentle expression turned dark when he looked at Beck, and he seemed to warn Beck to back off from his sister. Katelyn started to rush to Beck's defense—as if he would need defending.

Beck's features were equally dark, but when he received a phone call and glanced at the screen, fear seemed to swallow him whole.

"If you'll excuse me, I need to take this."

Heart pounding, he silently prayed for his son's safety. After the last twenty-four hours, he unfortunately wouldn't be surprised if Ollie had been targeted.

"Mom, what's up?" He tried to control the gruffness in his voice, but the moment he'd seen her number, his anxiety had jumped through the roof.

"Are you okay, Beck?" she asked. "You sound upset."

Her tone let him know his son was okay, and he slowly released his breath.

"I'm good. How's Ollie doing?" *Please just get to the reason for your call.* His attitude wasn't fair. She couldn't know what he'd been going through.

"Oh, he's fine. He has been playing outside with the neighbor's boy, Kurt."

He realized that Katelyn and crew were eyeing him so he moved out into the hallway. Her brother would probably take her to the station to look at the mug shots now. By the look in his eyes, Detective Bradley thought Beck was nothing but trouble.

Funny, he would be right about that, and if only he knew just how much trouble. Part of him wanted to put this all at the feet of law enforcement or special agents to handle, and Beck could simply brush off his hands and be done with it. But Beck had learned his lesson the hard way when he'd tried to tell the police. Honestly, he was surprised that he hadn't already been killed because of what he'd witnessed and believed and told the police. But then again, why go after the paranoid guy who believed a conspiracy theory about his wife? That would only make what he said ring true and law enforcement would then start digging deeper.

Yesterday everything had shifted when he'd made his discovery and now his life was on the line. He didn't want others' lives to be in danger. Katelyn would never forgive him if he dragged her brother into the danger, too, and something happened to him.

"Beck, hello? Are you still there?"

"Yes, Mom. Sorry. I'm with a friend and got distracted."

"Oh? What kind of friend, Beck?"

"Not that kind, Mom. Did you need something?" He hated sounding impatient, but he wished she would get to the reason for her call.

"I just wondered if you were going to pick Ollie up. Or we could bring him over?" Beck froze. He glanced at his watch. Was it that time already? How could he have forgotten?

"No, don't bring him. I'll come and get him in a couple of hours. That would save you the trouble."

"Oh, son, you know it's no trouble at all. We're happy to bring him over."

"Mom, please. I'm not at the house. I'll pick him up, but I need some time."

"Okay, that's fine. I'm only trying to help. But you should know that he's been asking me when *you're* going to take him to the picnic at the park like you promised."

Ollie meant everything to Beck, but he'd been consumed with finding answers to Mia's death and had left him with his parents. Beck trusted them entirely and had gotten lost in the happenings of the previous night and this morning. He was stumped as to how to respond, which told him his mind was still much too distracted.

What do I do about Ollie? How do I keep him

safe? Staying with Beck was not safe for Ollie right now.

"I thought perhaps we could just meet you there at the park. If you want to bring the chips, I'll bring the sandwiches. Oh, and I baked my million-dollar cookies."

Squeezing his eyes, he pinched the bridge of his nose. *Let me think. Let me think.*

How was he going to solve this while keeping both Ollie and his parents safe? He couldn't turn the clock back to close the box he'd opened that had led to the burglary and now two murder attempts on Katelyn's life.

Detective Bradley and Katelyn's partner, Ms. Peterson—soon to be Mrs. Bradley—stepped from the room. They hovered near Katelyn as if protecting her, and both gave him a severe look as they ushered her down the hallway, like they would take her to safety and far away from Beck. He hadn't officially hired her as a private investigator—no binding paperwork had been signed—and it looked like he was on his own, after all.

He preferred it that way and it was probably for the best, but on the other hand, did she realize she was still in danger? Had he convinced her the accident was no accident?

"Your breathing sounds funny, son." Dad now. "Are you okay? Your mother handed me the phone. You really should think about stopping that climbing business and join me at the hardware store. That door is always open."

"I know, Dad, and thanks."

"Daddy!" It sounded like Ollie had wrestled Mom's cell away. "Dad, let's go on that picnic. I helped Mimi bake the cookies and make sandwiches."

Beck's heart melted with love and he couldn't help but smile even in the middle of this nightmare. He couldn't deny his son anything. "Okay. Put Mimi back on the phone."

"Mom?"

"Yes, Beck."

"I'll meet you at the park at one thirty. It will mean a late lunch. Is that okay?"

"Perfect. We'll see you there."

Time with his family would ground him, and he definitely needed clarity. Maybe he could pay for a cruise to Alaska for them and get them far from town while he figured this out. He scratched his head. A woman cleared her throat.

He turned and found Katelyn dangling keys. "Tori is letting me borrow her car."

"I… Uh…" He thought she had left with her protective brother and friend.

She arched an eyebrow. "I don't think I've seen you speechless until this moment. I haven't decided if I like it or not." Katelyn turned and walked down the hallway, seemingly expecting him to join her. With the way she held herself, confident and strong, no one passing her in the hallway would ever know she'd just been in a car accident. Was that an act? Beck had been in the same car, and he was sure he appeared frazzled. He hadn't lost consciousness, so didn't need to be examined like Katelyn.

He caught up with her, still scrambling to shift his plans again.

"So who are we meeting at the park?" she asked.

"Honestly, I thought you were long gone by now."

She stopped and turned on him. Fisted her hands on her hips. "Gone? Where would I be going? I have a new case to solve."

"Yeah, about that..."

"You look indecisive about something. You can tell me about that on the way to the office to sign the PI paperwork."

"As I was saying, about that..." Was Katelyn better off getting back to her life? Maybe her attacker would back off if he had nothing to fear from Katelyn. Except she wouldn't let go. She was the only witness and had planned to look at mug shots.

Katelyn stepped closer and got in his face. Her pretty expression sobered. "Remember, I'm already in this and I'll be investigating with or without you. I told my brother and future sister-in-law nothing you've said to me. And about the accident you believe was deliberate, I'm willing to go with you on that. I'm here for you, Beck."

Beck hated to admit that he'd forgotten her earlier threat, but she'd acted on this new offer to help him as if she cared… And as if it was more than business. He had to be reading more into it. He hoped he was reading more into it, because Beck wasn't entirely sure he could resist this woman, even with his resolve that he wouldn't trust again.

"Now, tell me where we're going," she said.

Beck returned her smile. "To sign the PI paperwork and then to the park to eat sandwiches and chocolate-chip cookies and celebrate our new partnership."

"I love picnics." Katelyn offered a soft smile and laughed. "You're full of surprises, Beck Goodwin."

As are you, Katelyn. As are you.

He enjoyed the lyrical tones of her laughter entirely too much, especially with the danger breathing down their necks.

FIVE

A breeze whipped around her, tossing her hair into her eyes as she hiked through the grass next to Beck toward the picnic tables. A playground with a slide and swings was situated a few yards from the tables. Even though she'd grown up in this region of the country, she'd never actually been to this state park near the aptly named Castle Crags—the rocks jutting out of the spiking, lofty mountain looked exactly like a "craggy castle."

As she and Beck approached the tables and playground, an older couple stood. Katelyn recognized Oliver on the swing. He jumped and flew from the swing, landing on his feet. Without a break in his rhythm, he sprinted over to Beck.

The man picked him up and swung him around. "Hey, buddy. How you doing?"

Oliver giggled as Beck set him on the ground and shifted to tickling him. The boy's giggles sent warmth spreading out like a pebble dropped in a pond.

"Stop it!" He pulled away but kept laughing.

"Let's go try some of this grub you made." Beck pulled Oliver to him and knuckle-rubbed his head.

Oliver slipped out from his arm again and nearly tackled his father to the ground.

Myriad emotions surged through Katelyn. She couldn't pull her eyes from the pair. At the same time, her heart ached for their loss—Beck's wife and Oliver's mother—only a year ago.

Was it an accident or something much more nefarious, like Beck believed? Obviously, he had good reason to be suspicious of the past. If she let her thoughts go there, Katelyn could still feel that pillow pressed hard against her face so that she couldn't get any air. With a young boy in the mix, there was so much more at stake. Katelyn suddenly became aware of Beck's parents—she assumed—staring at her, questions in their eyes.

"Oh, excuse me." She thrust out her hand. "I'm Katelyn Bradley."

"It's nice to meet you, Katelyn. What a lovely name. I'm Marilyn Goodwin, Beck's mother, and this is my husband, Rayce."

Mr. Goodwin gave Katelyn a power shake. "Beck's dad. It's nice to meet you."

As if Katelyn wouldn't have recognized those same piercing eyes and strong jaw in Beck's father.

Mrs. Goodwin smiled and shook her head. "Beck never brings girls around. You're the first in quite some time."

Grief briefly flashed in the woman's eyes. Of course, Beck would grieve his wife. The mourning period was different for everyone, she'd heard. Some took months and others years. What would it take for Beck to get over the loss? Would he marry again soon for Oliver's sake, so he could have a mother, too? The boy was happy with his father—Beck was a good father, no doubt there.

Katelyn realized that Mrs. Goodwin was still waiting for an explanation from her. Beck's mother had the wrong idea about Katelyn's presence. She needed to set his parents straight, but she had no idea how much he'd told them about what was going on. Did they need to know she was a private investigator? Katelyn should have discussed this with Beck, during the drive over.

They had gone by the office space she shared with Tori for their private-investigations business. She'd snatched the paperwork from the printer just as Ryan called. While she talked, they'd gotten back into Beck's vehicle and headed straight for the park so they wouldn't be late.

Beck had that sense of urgency—a man on a mission to protect his son.

During the drive, Ryan had kept her on the phone, apprising her of the situation. They could return to their homes this afternoon. No evidence had been discovered so far. Then Ryan had started interrogating her about Beck and if she planned to work for him.

Katelyn hoped that Beck hadn't heard Ryan's side of the conversation. Ryan had advised her against working with Beck.

Yada. Yada. Who did her brother think he was, anyway? Katelyn had suspicions of her own, but she didn't want to share them with Ryan.

So she'd quickly changed the subject before the conversation got out of hand. "You sound like you have the wedding jitters, as some call it. Are you getting cold feet?"

"Of course not. I've loved Tori as long as I've known her. You know that. How could you even suggest such a thing?"

Ryan had protested too much, in Katelyn's opinion, and she figured she'd hit the mark, but that was his issue to process. At least Katelyn had successfully redirected the conversation with Beck listening in.

The next thing she knew Beck was pulling his vehicle into the state park.

He still hadn't signed the documents because her call had taken entirely too long.

"How long have you known our Beck?" Mr. Goodwin asked, bringing Katelyn back. How on earth would she set them straight?

Beck released Oliver and his eyes found hers and held her gaze. He'd heard his mother's question.

Rescue me! She hoped he could see the pleading in her eyes.

"How long have I known Beck?" she asked, stalling, as she moved toward him, hoping he would be the one to answer. "Well, we're neighbors and—"

"Katelyn was in a car wreck today." He put it out there so bluntly, Katelyn's mouth dropped open.

His mother and father both gasped.

"Oh, you poor girl," Mrs. Goodwin said.

"And I was only doing the neighborly thing by inviting her to our picnic." The way his eyes crinkled at the corners when he grinned, and those huge dimples around that great smile, made Katelyn's heart tumble against her rib cage.

"Well, you have to come to the table and sit

down. I take it you weren't terribly hurt." Mrs. Goodwin eyed Katelyn's forehead as she led them back to the picnic table. "Is that from the wreck? I didn't want to stare or be rude and ask about it."

The moment of the crash rushed over Katelyn as she eased onto the bench at the picnic table. Maybe she had pushed herself too soon to come here with Beck, but she would make up for it later. Find a safe place to rest.

She touched her head and winced. "Yes. I think my head hit the mirror or the airbag. I can't be sure."

"Oh, dear. You have a concussion?"

"I don't think so. I don't have a headache. I blacked out, though." Katelyn thought back to the moment she woke up in Beck's arms and wished she hadn't remembered—everyone was watching, including Beck. Was he thinking back, too?

Mr. Goodwin's expression showed his concern. "What happened?"

"Dad." Beck shook his head. He might have brought up the wreck as a means of explaining Katelyn's presence, but it was clear he didn't want to discuss the wreck in front of Oliver.

"Which sandwiches did you make, Ollie?" Beck asked.

"I'm sure Mimi's are better." Oliver laughed as he pointed at the bread. "I left fingerprints."

"Those are the best kind." Beck snatched two finger-printed sandwiches and handed one over to Katelyn. "Eat up. This guy is going to be a famous chef one day."

Oliver howled with laughter. Katelyn noticed Beck called him "Ollie" instead of Oliver.

Katelyn had to hand it to Beck. The man was under tremendous stress, but his son, his family, would never know it. She understood that. Beck wanted to protect Ollie—not just his physical well-being, but Beck didn't want his son to have any reason to be afraid. Admiration for him filled her. He put on a great show, for his family's sake, and yet, she knew that fear and anxiety hovered just beneath the surface. His gaze flicked to her briefly and she saw the hint of a warning there.

She hoped he knew that she would never give away his secret.

This time with his family, with his son, was too precious. But she worried that danger was quickly encroaching.

"I like Katelyn, Dad. I'm glad you brought her along. Is this a date?" Ollie moved to the end of the picnic table and grabbed three cookies before his grandmother could swat away his hands.

"Um, Katelyn is our neighbor, Ollie. Remember? And we're friends. She's your friend, too." Beck popped the rest of his sandwich in his mouth and winked at Katelyn.

She couldn't help but smile. She accepted the cookie Oliver offered and took a bite. After chewing, she said, "Yum, these are awesome. Did you make these, too?"

"I helped. Mimi's the cook. Dad knows there's no hope of me being a cook. But my momma was amazing." His expression soured as though he wished he hadn't thought of his mother.

Katelyn thought her heart might break.

"Mimi" lovingly swatted Oliver away from the cookies again. "That's enough for now. You go swing. I'll clean up."

Oliver headed for the swing set. Mrs. Goodwin eyed Beck, her face filled with love and concern for her son. "Beck, why don't you go for a walk with Katelyn. Your father and I'll clean up this mess. Then I suspect we should talk."

Beck shook his head. "We can help."

"Go on, son. I insist." Mr. Goodwin stood and started gathering trash.

Beck held his hand out to Katelyn. She couldn't say no to that look in his eyes and slipped her hand into his. Beck held her hand as they walked, and Katelyn wasn't entirely sure why. Nor was she certain why she left her hand in his, but while she did, she felt the strength in his grip along with that buzzing electric sensation that seemed constant between them.

Like someone caught in an electrical current, she was powerless to free herself.

Katelyn's hand was soft and, at the same time, strong in his, and he was acutely aware of her presence, as well as the eyes on his back as they left his parents and Ollie behind.

"I thought you wanted your family to think we're just friends."

He squeezed her hand, then slowly released it, and instantly wished he'd held on to her hand a little longer.

When he could find his voice, he said, "I do. But friends can mean different things. I know my family well enough to know that if we pretended there was nothing more between us, they would ask more questions. I don't want questions right now. This way, they'll give me space."

So basically he'd just admitted to her that there was more between them. As if she didn't already know. But he admitted to her that he felt it, too. Not that the "more between them" could ever grow into anything permanent, but there was no point in playing games or dancing around the obvious—not with lives at stake.

Katelyn said nothing and he assumed she understood his reasoning. Nor did she seem to object to his comment about "friends" meaning different things.

They reached a copse of evergreens next to the river. Beck allowed the familiar sound of rushing water to soothe his nerves. It was as if it was smoothing away the rough edges, polishing, like he was a pebble or a rock resting in the flowing river. Sometimes he wished he could be that unmoving, and not tossed to and fro as life came at him hard and fast.

Standing here with Katelyn and watching the river in silence, Beck realized it was a comfortable silence and he didn't have to put on a show or "airs" with Katelyn. He could completely be himself, and right now, she was the only one close to him who knew what was going on. Except she didn't know the details, and he wished she wasn't involved because it was dangerous to her. But there was no denying he appreciated having someone else in this with him.

Beck lifted his gaze from the river to the rocky outcroppings of the nearby Castle Crags. With twenty-foot cliffs and nine-hundred-foot spires, the granite domes and walls were great for climbing. Most of the climbing was easy, but there were a few places that could be a challenge even for experienced climbers. He spotted three figures climbing the Castle Dome on the side that was a fourth-class route.

"See the people up there?" He pointed.

Katelyn peered upward across the river toward the crags, exposing her lovely long neck. She shaded her eyes and nodded. Beck forced his gaze back to where it should be.

"This is where I come to train rock climbers. Usually not beginners, though. I'll take a small group out and we work on the basic skills they've already acquired."

"You sound like you love your job, Beck."

He sighed. "I do. It's my business and I do it because I don't know what else I would do." He had no idea how growing up with a dad who owned a hardware store had led to Beck's love of the outdoors, but maybe it was simply he lived close enough to fall in love. He'd started right at the Castle Crags.

She dropped her gaze to the river. "What are we doing here? Aren't you concerned about bringing danger to your family?"

"I am."

"Why don't you tell them?"

"I will." He'd taken this time to think about his next step. How he could keep them safe. "When we go back, I'll talk them into taking

Ollie on a camping trip for a few days. That should buy us some time."

"Us. You're sure you want to work with me? You haven't signed that paperwork yet."

"I will. And, yes, I'm sure. As you've warned me several times already, you're investigating with or without me."

"Usually as a private investigator I investigate *for* people. Not *with* them."

"I think you know that won't work this time."

A tenuous smile emerged on her face. Beck had to force his eyes from her lips, which he instinctively knew were soft. He needed to get control over his attraction to her that went much deeper than simply physical. There was so much at stake. He tried to shake off the effect her presence had on him.

"I know," she said. "So why don't you go ahead and tell me. At this rate, it will be the end of the week before you can show me."

"I hope I can show you today, but you're right. I had planned to show you this afternoon, but then Mom called. I had to be here for Ollie. I needed to see that he's all right, and then urge them to leave town."

"That makes sense. Now tell me what's going on."

Beck plopped down on the grass next to a tree, and Katelyn joined him.

"We can talk here and nobody will bother us."

Katelyn eyed his family as if she was as concerned about them as he was.

"Don't worry, they're safe there for the moment. We're safe." Beck said the words but he had a feeling that he hadn't fooled Katelyn, and she somehow knew that tension rolled through his muscles. He was ready to pounce, ready to protect at the slightest hint of danger. All his senses were on high alert.

"Okay, Beck. I'm waiting to hear your story."

He drew in a long breath. He hadn't spoken of this with anyone else. Doubts accosted him but he plowed forward. "I met Mia on a rock-climbing world tour. She was a climber, as well. We fell in love and married quickly. Ollie came along not long after. We had been the perfect couple and became a happy family. I'd wanted to grow our family. I stopped touring and settled down for Mia and Ollie, and that's when I started working as a trainer. Plenty of people wanted to train under me. I turned down offers to take groups on guided tours to some of the toughest canyons and mountains so I could be close to my family."

"And Mia, was she happy, as well?"

"She seemed blissful at first, and then I sensed something different about her. She was on edge. I couldn't help but feel like she was hiding something. We were so close and I knew something was wrong. She wouldn't tell me. I loved her so much and I didn't want to smother her or stifle her. I didn't want to act like a possessive and jealous jerk."

Katelyn eyed him. "But you did, anyway."

"I didn't think I was, but she accused me of those things. She accused me of being paranoid."

"Do you ever think you might have been just that? Paranoid? That you're being paranoid even now?"

He heard the insinuation in her tone—and her unspoken suggestion he should see a doctor. "There's nothing wrong with getting help so I agreed to see a marriage counselor, only Mia was the one to refuse. Still, even without counseling, everything improved for a while, but then she lied to me. I followed her and spotted her meeting with someone."

"Meeting. What does that mean? She could have been meeting someone for any number of reasons. Did something happen between them?"

"Not then. Not that I saw, but it shook me up pretty bad. It was then that I became a crazed jealous husband, at least on the inside. I kept it all to myself…for Ollie's sake. For our family's sake."

"From what I've seen of your interaction with

your family today, I believe you could actually pull that off."

"I watched her. I found…a gun. She had a gun she never told me about." He covered his face for a moment, then dropped his hands when he remembered his family was watching. "I started to suspect that she was a federal agent."

"What? You mean…undercover?"

"Undercover or more like a spy. When Ollie was five, she started traveling for her job."

"Wait. What did she do other than climb rocks?"

"She worked for an outdoors company, then became a buyer and traveled. At least that's what she told me. I confronted her one night when she returned from a trip. I'd—I'd had enough. But she had this power over me—"

"You mean love. She loved you and you loved her."

He nodded. "I gave in and as she held me, she whispered in my ear that she would tell me everything."

Katelyn shifted to cross her legs, her eyes riveted to him as he told the story. He could hardly believe he was telling anyone all of this. Just laying it all out there to this woman who he didn't know that well. A stranger, for all practical purposes.

"The next day I'd come down from a training

session and I found a note in my locker—Mia would meet me for dinner at our favorite restaurant. She was going to tell me everything. She had arranged for my parents to watch Ollie for the evening. She was so secretive and on edge—but I knew—" he held Katelyn's gaze "—I knew that she loved me, and that she was somehow in trouble and had been protecting me and Ollie the whole time."

Beck didn't say more but watched Katelyn. Was she tracking with him? Believing him? He couldn't understand why her opinion, her belief in him, was so important to him at this moment. His throat grew dry, making it hard to form his next words.

He squeezed his eyes to block the emotions that suddenly rolled through him—he remembered that night as if it had happened mere seconds before.

"I'd arrived at the restaurant anxious to see her. I wanted to help her with whatever this was that she'd gotten herself into. I wanted to stop it from coming between us." He released a ragged breath. "I spotted her car as it crossed a short bridge over a river. An oncoming truck was going slowly and it suddenly sped up and crashed into her car, crumpling it before my eyes. If that wasn't enough, it continued forward and pushed her vehicle through the guardrail and into the river."

Katelyn pressed her hand over his, and he soaked up the comfort she offered. "I'm so sorry, Beck. So sorry."

To her credit, she didn't interrupt him with questions, but gave him the space to process through the emotions. Somehow, she seemed to sense how much was roiling around inside him.

"I jumped into the river after her. Swam down to try to free—" He caught himself as his voice choked. He couldn't speak with those traumatic images in his mind.

After a few moments, he regained his composure. "I told the police what I'd seen and that the vehicle had intentionally sped up. That someone had deliberately rammed her and then driven away. I told them she was about to tell me the truth, but I'm sure you can imagine how they interpreted things. For a while, they even suspected me of hiring someone to kill her because I was a jealous husband who suspected her of having an affair."

He hung his head, hating to relive everything, but now was the moment when he had to share it all, and he thanked God that Katelyn was kindhearted and understanding, and the person to help him.

"For a while, I had to put it all behind me for

Ollie's sake. He'd lost his mother at only seven. He needed normalcy, not a crazy paranoid father. So I told myself the police were right and Mia's accusations were right—I was too possessive and had become jealous."

"But deep inside you knew differently." Her tone was gentle and reassuring.

"After six months had passed, I allowed myself to review everything and I knew I was right all along. Besides, Mia loved me, and she wasn't going to break off our marriage that night. I've been making a few phone calls here and there. Tried to talk to someone from her company to find out more about her job and travels."

"And?"

"That company never existed."

SIX

His words knocked the breath from Katelyn, and she drew in air. More than anything, she wanted to believe him on every account. The Beck she'd come to know in a short time was full of love and self-control. Mia had been a fortunate woman to have found a man like him. But she suspected there was much more to this story and Katelyn decided that she was in this with Beck for the long haul, however long it took.

"Tell me what you found in your house, Beck."

"I suspected that Mia could have hidden something in our home. We lived in an apartment, and then when she became pregnant we bought a home to fill with love." He was quiet for a few heartbeats, then said, "When we first moved in, I worked to remodel, renovating and upgrading, like anyone does in an old home, but then when I became suspicious of her, I used that as an excuse to search for anything she could have hidden. I thought I was probably grasping at straws or losing it, but I had to try. It was the only way to keep me—" He cleared his throat. "To keep my sanity."

He gave her a look that seemed to beg her not to think him crazy.

Katelyn pressed her hand over his to reassure him and sat taller. "You found something in the house?"

He subtly nodded. "After she died, I kept working, again, to keep my sanity. Two nights ago, I found a safe behind a wall in the basement. I hadn't worked on remodeling down there, but had focused on the main floor. The wall had been painted in such a way so it would look old and match the rest of the basement. Once I looked close enough, I could tell it was new and had been installed since we'd moved in—right under my nose! We'd been living in the home for years. So it wasn't that hard. When I found the safe, I knew it must contain information Mia wanted hidden. Kept secret from others including me, her husband. Or maybe she would have shared everything—including the fact she'd had a safe installed in our home—that night if she hadn't been murdered."

He hung his head.

Katelyn gave him the time he needed.

"I took Ollie to stay with my parents the next

day after school. To keep up the ruse that everything was normal, I had to stay for dinner, and then played a few video games with Ollie. I stopped by a hardware store to get a variety of tools I might need to open the safe. Just in case. When I got home I heard noises down in the basement. I found someone down there. He fought me and fled, and then I chased him back up and fought with him. I wanted to know who he was and get answers. I'm embarrassed that he got the best of me."

"And I stepped in to save the day." She offered him a grin. "I know you didn't want me involved, but, Beck, if what you're telling me is the correct interpretation of the events, then that burglar could have killed you."

He shrugged. "He came for the safe. I don't think he was going to kill me initially, but then after I chased him and we ended up in the library, I think he made his decision to get rid of me. I know I didn't act like I appreciated what you did, but I do. You probably saved my life last night."

"You're welcome. Thank you for saving mine, too."

"I guess that makes us even." He stared at her as though he might chuckle, but none of it was funny. "It took me too long to figure out that someone must have planted bugs or cameras in the house after Mia died, waiting for the moment when I would discover whatever Mia had hidden. Once I did, he came in to retrieve the items from the safe. Once those items were gone, I would have nothing to back up my claims that Mia had been murdered." He sighed. "Once again I would look like a paranoid fool if I tried to go to the police."

"Except that didn't happen, Beck. I was there and I saw the guy. Things have obviously escalated, with the attack on me. Since I've seen the man's face, I still need to go in to look at those mug shots, but I don't hold out any hope he's in them—I mean, if this is really cloak-and-dagger spy stuff." She tried not to make it sound like she was making a joke. "And in that case, I can meet with a sketch artist, but first I want to see that safe."

He nodded and pushed to his feet, offering Katelyn his hand. She didn't want to become addicted to the feel of his grip, or even that surge of energy that shot through her at his touch. She had a feeling that was exactly what would happen. Beck stirred longings in her heart, and she thought she had more control over those feelings. So she pushed to her feet without his help.

She eyed Beck's family, still at the picnic table. Ollie was on the slide. "What now?" This was his show, after all.

"Now, we go back to the table. You swing my son for me while I talk to my parents. I'll only tell them enough to let them know to be wary of strangers or danger. Mom suspects something already. She's always been able to read me."

Katelyn walked with Beck back to the picnic table, only this time they didn't hold hands—his parents noticed, but said nothing.

Mrs. Goodwin rose and smiled at them both. "There's a few more cookies left. Please eat them up so I don't need to pack them." She opened the plastic container and offered the cookies. "Everything okay?"

"I'm going to hang out with Ollie." Katelyn smiled, then left Beck to speak with his parents.

She approached the playground. Ollie had lost interest in the slide and was now crouching and playing with a stick.

"What are you looking at?" She squatted next to him.

"Oh, just a cricket."

"Mind if I hang out with you? We could swing."

"I guess so." Ollie left the cricket to return to its business and raced to beat her to the swings.

He scrambled on and started rocking back and forth until he propelled his swing so high she was afraid he would fall out.

She was slower to get into the swing next to

him, barely fitting her rear into it. She smiled at Ollie and started kicking her way to swinging high like him—something she used to do as a kid. But her insides went queasy now. She glanced at Beck and noted the serious expression on his face. His parents had their backs to Katelyn and Ollie so she couldn't see if their faces reflected his somber appearance.

Ollie slowed his swing, then flew out of it, landing on his feet.

"Ollie, wait!" Katelyn hoped to prevent him from interrupting Beck's conversation, but she was too late. He took off to the picnic table.

Beck smiled and wrapped his arm around Ollie. Katelyn watched as she made her way toward them. Ollie frowned and shrugged. What was that about? Everyone rose from the table as she approached.

"What's going on?"

Beck's intense gray eyes held her gaze. "Ollie's going camping with Mom and Dad."

The kid didn't appear all that excited about the news. Katelyn guessed he wanted to come home and spend more time with his dad, and she so got that. Beck was a special kind of guy. She'd have to be an idiot not to see that.

"Baseball just ended, Ollie. This is the perfect time for you to hang out with Pops and Mimi."

"But you're not going to be there."

Beck ruffled Ollie's dark hair—he must take after his mother, Mia, in that department. "I know, but I have to work. And I promise once I finish, if I can, I'll join you at the campsite."

Ollie jerked his head to Katelyn. "Will our new friend come, too?"

Beck's chuckle sounded forced as he glanced at her. "I don't know, Ollie."

"I need to get my fishing pole and my DS."

"You don't need electronics." The man looked to his mother for help.

Mrs. Goodwin rose from the table. "Come on, Ollie. We have enough clothes for you. You don't need to make a trip home. Pops has an extra fishing pole or we can buy one. We plan on heading out as soon as possible."

Mrs. Goodwin hugged Beck and kissed him on both cheeks. "You be careful now."

She eyed Katelyn and smiled, then shook her hand, pressing it between both of hers. "I'm so glad you're here for Beck."

Katelyn tried to absorb the heartfelt thanks and maybe with it she could get a sense of just what Beck might have told his mother. A lot? Or very little?

Ollie trudged off with his grandparents, leaving Katelyn more than curious. "Just what *did* you tell them?"

"Everything."

Katelyn felt her jaw drop again. She'd thought Beck had intended to hold something back. "Wait. Everything?"

"Yes."

"But why?"

"I realized they weren't going to settle for half truths."

Beck frowned as he watched them get into their SUV and quickly drive away. He waved at his son as the SUV headed around the park to the exit, then turned his full attention on Katelyn.

"What did they say?" she asked. "How did they respond?"

"They think I need help."

Back in town, Beck took Katelyn to the county sheriff's offices. He waited while she sat at a desk in the corner and looked through stacks of mug shots. Katelyn didn't see the intruder in the photographs. Beck hadn't thought she would, but they'd needed to get that out of the way. The county forensic artist was recovering from surgery, so it would be next week before Katelyn would meet with him.

Then it was on to the moment they had both been waiting for—when Beck would show Katelyn the safe. He parked his vehicle at the curb down the street from his house instead of in the driveway, or even in front.

"Why are you parking here?"

"Just want to hang back and see if anyone is lurking about."

Katelyn said nothing to that, but he knew she had more she wanted to say. She had kept quiet during the drive back and he appreciated her sensitivity. He tried to rise above how profoundly his parents' reaction affected him. They hadn't exactly come out and said they didn't believe him, but he saw it plain as day in their eyes. Mom had asked him several times about seeing her counselor friend. She and Dad both thought that Beck had suffered some sort of emotional break with reality since Mia's death. His biggest fear where they were concerned was that they could possibly try to take Ollie away from him—but then again, his parents knew that Ollie would have none of that. Beck was good for Ollie, and he loved his son dearly.

Still, it broke his heart when at the table today his mother had reached over, taken his hand and said, "For your son's sake, Beck, please, can't you see this is only going to make things worse?"

He released a long and heavy sigh that Katelyn couldn't have missed, but she didn't comment. Now he was curious about what she was thinking. But he could wait her out. He didn't trust himself to speak just yet, anyway.

Katelyn shifted to look at him. "Okay, well, under normal circumstances this would be the moment I should say thank you for an interesting day. Then I would get out and head home. But I want to see what all the fuss is about, and what someone has tried to kill me twice over."

He turned to face her. Took in her lovely features. Soft smile, and amazing eyes. That hair. *Careful, Beck.* "Thanks for that, Katelyn."

"To some degree, I know what you're going through—I mean, how hard it is when others don't believe in you. You begin to second-guess everything. To doubt yourself." Katelyn gazed off into the distance like she was far from him as she spoke.

"Sometime, I'd like to hear *your* story."

"My story?" She jerked her gaze to him.

"What happened to you before that helps you to understand what I'm going through right now."

Her smile was tenuous. "I can't truly understand, but I'm trying."

"You have no idea how much that means to me," Beck said. "Now let me sign those papers and we'll go look at the safe."

The private-investigator contract signed, they hiked down the street and tromped up the front walk. Would Clara be watching? At the front door, Katelyn brandished her weapon. "Let's make sure it's safe inside the house and no one is waiting for us."

"I have my own gun." Beck tugged his gun from the small holster at his waist. Carrying a concealed weapon was a new and necessary habit for him. "But you're the ex-cop who knows more about how to wield a deadly weapon. You first then." He gestured for her to take the lead because he knew she wanted that. She appeared to be in her element and he wouldn't take the moment from her.

She was definitely a take-charge woman and he loved that about her.

Once they were sure no one was in the home, Beck tucked his gun away. "He doesn't need to be here in the house to hear us and see us."

"You mean the bugs."

"I do."

"Let's exterminate them. You take that side of the house, I'll take this side."

"Um, I don't exactly have a lot of experience with this. What am I looking for?"

"I know a little about it." Her shrug was cute. "I don't use bugs or cameras in the PI business, don't get the wrong idea." She explained what he should look for and they each scoured the home.

Katelyn found a small camera in the living room. "That was it."

"I found a listening device in my bedroom. Guess the police weren't exactly looking for bugs and cameras. Just prints and any DNA left behind by the intruder."

"Right. And there could still be more that *we* missed," she said.

"I figure that we have limited time before someone else shows up here. The doors are locked and the alarm is armed."

Katelyn shoved back her hair and twisted it into a ponytail. "Okay, so show me the safe."

Beck led her down a hallway and into the basement. He hadn't found any bugs or cameras down here, but that didn't mean anything. What difference did it make at this juncture, since the safe had already been discovered? He feared that the contents had already been stolen. At the wall, he removed the Sheetrock that he'd put back in place to hide the safe.

"Now that we're looking at it, any chance you know how to open it?"

"I've tried birth dates and anniversaries." He frowned. "Any suggestions?"

"We could hire someone to open it," she said.

"That would be my last choice."

"It might be your only choice." Katelyn glanced around the basement. "Let's do a little research about this kind of safe and how we could break it open."

He chuckled.

"People learn how to build bombs on the internet. I wouldn't be surprised if we could learn how to open this safe without the combination."

"The internet connection isn't so great down here. Let's go upstairs. I'm parched. We can get a drink while we research." Once upstairs, Beck shut all the mini blinds. "Don't want anyone looking in."

Katelyn glanced through a slat in one of the blinds. "I don't see any suspicious vehicles out there. The sooner we get this over with, the better."

Beck poured a glass of milk and offered it to her.

Katelyn frowned. "Got any chocolate syrup?"

"I have an eight-year-old." He grabbed the syrup and handed it to Katelyn. "Of course I do."

He watched her pour syrup into her milk and then laughed. "You're as bad as Ollie. I have to do it or he abuses the privilege."

She smiled and winked, then drank from the glass, her eyes never leaving his. He downed his milk and wiped away the residual moustache. *Time to get busy.* While Katelyn used her cell phone to search for information, he focused on his laptop, which was open at the kitchen counter. He was very aware of Katelyn Bradley's every move. Every breath. Every twitch of her nose. Every pucker of her lips.

Katelyn Bradley was quickly getting under his skin.

He reminded himself that Mia, whether for the right reasons or the wrong reasons, had lied to him and acted duplicitously. No one could ever truly be trusted, including Beck. He hoped that Katelyn knew she shouldn't trust him.

Lost in his thoughts about Katelyn, he didn't realize she'd moved from her position until she hovered much too near and looked over his shoulder. "So I have a question. What happens if we open the safe and we find…nothing?"

He whirled in the chair. "What do you mean if we find nothing?"

"You're hinging everything on what's in the safe, Beck. What if there's nothing—nothing in the safe? Then what?"

He frowned. "It could mean that someone already got to the safe and took everything."

"Or it could mean there was nothing in there to begin with. Who owned this house before you? Could be it belonged to someone else and the information wasn't passed along to you by the Realtor or the previous owner."

"The safe and its hiding spot are all new. I explained that." And he thought she believed him.

"Is there any chance you could be wrong about that? Even the slightest chance?"

"Nope."

"Okay, so what happens if we open the safe and you find something…incriminating? Or even something to prove that Mia was a government agent. Then what?"

"I don't know."

"I do. We need to give the information to the authorities."

"You mean the police."

"I'm sorry, but yes. What else can you do with it? You're trying to prove that someone killed Mia. You can't do that on your own."

"I'm not doing it on my own. I hired you, remember?"

Her ponytail sagging, Katelyn weaved her fingers through her hair. "Beck, I'm not the police. I can investigate but at the end of the day the information—especially incriminating information—will need to be handed over."

"Don't forget, I tried telling the police before."

"Before you had any actual evidence. I'm just trying to establish some game rules here. Or rather ground rules. We find something. We turn it over."

"You mean to your brother." Beck shoved from the counter and paced his kitchen, loathing that he seemed to be doing that an awful lot lately. "I thought we'd already addressed this and you were on board with it. Katelyn, you're in danger. You've already experienced that. Each person you tell will then be in danger."

"You told your parents."

"Because they need to know in order to keep Ollie safe." He rubbed his temples. "We need to get into that safe. In the meantime, act normal. Like everything's normal. Even to your brother."

"How am I supposed to ask questions and investigate? That's why you hired me, remember?"

Beck pressed his palms against the counter and leaned forward, hanging his head.

"Beck." She touched his back. "Why don't you just move and leave the safe, leave it all behind?"

He turned to face her. He couldn't help it. He gently grabbed her shoulders. "Whoever was behind killing my wife, whoever was behind the attack in my home and on you, will keep coming. Don't you get it? I have to know what's inside that safe. I have to know the truth in order to protect those I care about."

With the words, Beck knew that he cared

deeply about Katelyn, deeper than he had a right to. With the shimmer in her gaze, Katelyn knew that, too.

She slowly nodded. "For everyone's sake, I want you to know the truth, too. Let's go break into that safe."

SEVEN

With growing exasperation, Katelyn pressed her head against the safe and groaned. She'd tried to find the combination, using the techniques she'd read about, but it remained locked. She dropped her hands and growled, then marched away from the stupid safe.

"I don't get it! I've tried this ten times and I still can't open it. It shouldn't be this hard. What am I doing wrong?" She stretched out her arm and opened up her palm. "I think we should hire someone. We're wasting time trying to do this ourselves."

Beck's face remained stone, but a scowl brewed behind his gaze. "I'll give it a try."

She knew he didn't want to hire someone, but this was ridiculous. "You've already tried, remember? We're done. This is taking too long, Beck."

He approached the safe and stared at it.

"So it's in the wall, but is it heavy to lift?" she asked.

"Why do you ask?"

"We can move it out of here. Take it somewhere to get it open." She threw her arms up and let them drop. "I don't know."

Katelyn understood why Beck couldn't trust anyone else with this. Trusting could be both dangerous to Katelyn and Beck, as well as to the person charged with opening the safe. She didn't need him to tell her again that getting the police involved at this juncture would only muddy the waters.

She was with him—they had to find some hard evidence, no matter how small, to support Beck's theories about Mia. That would help them stop the madness…and keep them safe. But, honestly, she was more worried about Ollie.

At some point, she feared this would come back to him—the most precious person in Beck's life. But she kept those words to herself. No doubt, he had already considered that even sending Ollie away wouldn't stop someone who was determined. In fact, with that thought in mind, she could almost wish that whoever was after the contents of the safe had already retrieved them. Maybe the danger would be over for them.

Beck had pressed his ear against the safe

again. He was going to try figuring out the combination.

While he worked on the safe, she pressed her back against the wall and rubbed the tension in her shoulders.

She could hardly believe any of this was happening. If she told Ryan, he would insist she back away and drop the case. Ryan trusted her, but only to a point. He was protective, and she got that. He definitely wouldn't want her getting involved in something so cloak-and-dagger. And that was just it; Katelyn wanted to believe Beck with everything inside her. Sure, she'd been attacked in her own home, but that could be for the simple reason she'd seen the man behind the mask. That did not necessarily mean that car accident was something more. It didn't mean that attacker was after the safe, or that Mia was a spy and someone had killed her.

Admittedly, all that could be in Beck's imagination. Beck believed it, and for now, that was good enough for Katelyn. She would work alongside him and push away the doubt.

But what if she was wrong? What if Beck was actually suffering from mental illness and he was clinically paranoid? She had to consider that reality. The Beck she'd spent the last day with appeared as lucid as anyone she'd ever met. He was strong and trustworthy. Loved his family.

But was her heart simply wishing what he said was true because she'd been so hurt in the past?

She sighed. She was no professional if she allowed the events of her past to color her work so spectacularly. Regardless of professionalism, it was because of that hurt that she would do well to ignore her attraction to him—that strong emotional connection that bordered on being overwhelming, as well as that ping of energy that zinged through her every time she got too close. The attraction was nearly impossible to ignore.

But all things were possible with God, and—*God, help me*—with His help, she could resist Beck Goodwin.

An alarm sounded somewhere, only it was muffled. Was that coming from outside? Some other house?

Katelyn stiffened. "Beck, you hear that?"

"Quiet," he barked. "You know I can't do this if you're going to talk."

She doubted he could do it, anyway. They had both tried. They would never succeed in the safe-cracking business.

Katelyn headed for the steps out of the basement and as she neared the door, a pungent odor slammed her.

"Smoke, I smell smoke! Beck—it's the smoke alarms!"

He stumbled away from the safe, a deer-in-the-headlights look in his eyes. "Let's get out of here!"

Katelyn grabbed the knob and twisted.

The door was locked!

Beck's insides twisted into a tangled, painful knot. He could smell the smoke, too.

Please let it not be my house that's burning. Though wishing that on someone else wasn't something Beck wanted, either.

Katelyn stepped aside. Beck grabbed the doorknob and twisted. Stupid, stupid! He shook the knob until his hands ached. Frustration boiled up and he pounded on the door as if someone was on the other side and would come and help them. As if the person who had locked them inside would quickly unlock the door because Beck wanted out.

"What happened? Why won't it open?"

He ground his molars to keep from blurting out what he thought should be obvious to Katelyn, but maybe she didn't want to admit it and was hoping he would offer up another explanation for why they were locked in the basement. If he told her what he thought, he would only sound paranoid. He wanted Katelyn to come to her own conclusions, or at least be the first one to say what they were both thinking.

The only explanation was that they had been locked down here deliberately. Whoever locked them in had also set the house on fire.

"Beck, why don't you answer me? What are we going to do?" Katelyn's panicked voice yanked back his focus.

"Give me a second."

He pressed the heels of his palms into his eyes. Why was this happening? If the attacker couldn't get at the safe, then he didn't want anyone else getting into it, either, and discovering the contents. That had to be it. But again, if he said those words out loud he would sound like he'd lost his grip on reality...even to himself.

None of that mattered at this moment. Fear swelled in his chest and he glanced at Katelyn. He couldn't stand to see that same fear reflected in her eyes.

"It's going to be okay. We're going to get out of here." He projected a confidence he didn't feel as he bounded down the steps.

"Oh, yeah? How?" Katelyn was right behind him.

He searched through the construction materials. Plywood and tools. Hammers, nails, screwdrivers. Power tools. Brooms, mops and rakes clustered together in a corner.

That was it.

He stepped over boxes and a power saw and searched the random tools for one in particular.

An ax. The was the tool of firemen. Beck gripped the old rusty thing he'd found in the basement when he'd cleaned it out, grateful he hadn't tossed it yet, thinking it had no value for him.

Beck lifted the ax and stared at the rusted head. "This should work."

Alarms continued to sound in the house. He hoped the fire department was already here and dousing the place with water, and that firemen were already working their way through the house to see if any unfortunate soul had been caught inside and was unconscious on the floor.

He glanced at beautiful Katelyn. He would not wait in hopes they would be found in time. He couldn't trust that the fire department had been called at all. Clara, the neighborhood watchdog, could be visiting her son, out for dinner with friends, or running an errand.

Katelyn's eyes widened when he lifted the ax and turned toward her.

"Move out of the way."

She quickly moved out of his path as he ran back up the steps. The door was at a landing at the bottom of another set of stairs. "I'll try to hack open the door, but we can't be sure we'll find a way out."

There, he'd told her the truth. He hadn't sugarcoated their options.

"Okay. You do that. I'll try to break open one of the windows and call for help since our cells are useless down here."

Creating an escape window, bringing all the windows to code, had been on his to-do list. This older home had no such window.

Sweat beaded at his temples as he lifted the ax and drove the rusty blade into the thick wood, glad this door wasn't galvanized steel like his front door. The ax landed in the wood, the action jolting him all the way up his arms to his shoulders. He'd splintered a portion of the door.

He lifted the ax and continued hacking at the door, creating some cracks. The blare of the smoke alarm, no longer muffled, now emphasized their treacherous predicament.

Now that he thought about it, he hadn't closed the door while they were down here, and he didn't think Katelyn had, either. The idea that someone had crept through the house and down the steps to shut the basement door—and lock it—without them even being aware chilled him to the core. Ignited his fury.

He wouldn't let whoever was after this safe hurt Katelyn.

Beck chopped, chopped, chopped at the door. Wood splintered everywhere, but he kept chopping.

"Beck. Beck... Beck!" Katelyn's voice broke through the chaos in his mind.

Panting for breath, he dropped the ax at his feet on the top step, along with pieces of wood.

"The door is dead," she said. "No need to keep hacking."

He stared through the hole he'd opened up in the door at the glowing landing. "I'm not sure we can get out this way."

There were no good options.

Beck needed to pray. He was angry and hurt, and he didn't feel like he could face the Almighty in that condition, but now he was also desperate.

Lord, please help me save her!

"Help! Can someone hear me? Help us!" Katelyn was still at the window. She shouted through the opening that was much too small to escape out of.

But how could anyone help them, even if they heard her cries? Beck was done deliberating about what to do next. It was time for action, so he went back down the steps.

"We have to face the flames, Katelyn. It's the only way. I'll go up and check it out first."

Katelyn grabbed his arm. "No. You can't."

"I can't let you die here."

EIGHT

Beck shrugged out of her grip. Katelyn watched, disbelieving, as he clomped up the steps toward the hacked open door. He carefully stepped through the jagged, splintered opening.

"Beck, wait! Please don't go up there."

He glanced over his shoulder and peeked back through the opening, looking as if he didn't expect to see her again. Then he continued rising up the stairs until he disappeared into the smoke-filled, glowing, crackling house.

"Are you crazy?" she shouted.

The words had slipped out before she'd caught them. But he was definitely crazy. Still, they had no choice but to try to escape.

Katelyn had no idea if this was the way to go about it, nor did she have the time needed to figure it out. The fire was eating away at the house and getting closer to taking their lives. If they stayed in the basement, eventually the roof above would cave in on top of them—that is, depending on how out of control the fire had gotten.

If the fact that she was already drenched in sweat was any indicator, she might only have a few more moments to live. And in that case, she would die trying.

Here goes nothing. Or everything.

Katelyn took one step forward.

Lord, You say when I pass through the waters, You will be with me. When I pass through the rivers they won't sweep over me. So now when I pass through the fire, I will not be burned. The flames will not set me ablaze. Let that be true right now. Please protect us!

She took another step. Then another, repeating the verses in her head to give her strength.

Smoke had engulfed the stairwell up to the first floor, and she stepped through the splintered door, into the thick layer of toxic, noxious air.

"Beck!"

Katelyn coughed, but fear choked her even more. Her knees shook. She couldn't go any farther. To do so would mean her death. Beck… Was he already dead?

Pain exploded in her heart at the thought. Why had he gone up there? To try to save her? Beck had tried to save them both, but he couldn't have survived.

Katelyn's knees shook and she couldn't breathe.

Oh, Lord... When I pass—

Just as she thought she would crumple, a blanketed form rushed out of nowhere toward her. The blanket lifted.

Beck. The strong mountain-climbing man had returned. He yanked the blanket from his body, revealing another blanket underneath, and wrapped her in it before she could protest. The blanket was cool and wet. He kept the other one over himself.

Still, she tried. "Wait! What are you doing?" Coughs racked through her again. No more words could come from her raw, hoarse throat. Beck coughed, too. Neither of them could talk about this until they were out of here.

Wrapped like this, she wasn't going anywhere, so she stopped fighting. He'd wrapped her before she had a chance to comprehend what he was doing and act on it.

Beneath the wet blanket over his head, he'd covered his mouth and nose with a scarf, and his gaze pierced hers. Fear boiled behind his gray eyes. Fear and determination.

If anyone could get them out of this, Beck was the one person to do it. Beck covered her face, then grabbed her up into his arms and held her against his chest as he climbed back up the stairs. She was wrapped in a cold, wet cocoon.

She buried her face in the blanket and squeezed her eyes shut. Willing Beck to get them out. Willing them to be okay. Willing strength into his limbs and breath into his lungs.

Thank You, God. Beck is the one You sent to walk us through the fires.

She pushed down the panic and calmed her breathing. He was risking his life for her to get her out of here. Pops and cracks filled her ears and closed in on her from every side. Even the cold, wet blanket grew warmer as Beck held her tight against his lean, strong physique, grunting and groaning and coughing. She sensed the tension and anguish rippling through him as he tried to find them a way out.

Fear engulfed her—were they doomed from the start?

Suddenly Beck seemed to stumble. Katelyn braced herself for crashing against a flame-lit wall, but Beck rushed forward. Glass shattered and he tumbled to the ground, then rolled to protect Katelyn. Still, they hit the ground hard and pain ignited through her body as the limited air in her lungs rushed away.

But it was nothing—relief filled her. They were out of the house. Out of the fire and certain death.

Beside her, Beck coughed and hacked.

Her eyes burned and she couldn't open them. She wanted to see him. To see that he was okay and not burned or injured. But she was powerless to unwrap herself. Katelyn drew in the fresh air. Though it smelled smoky, it was certainly not toxic, like what they'd encountered in the house.

"A little help here?" She croaked out the words, sounding weak and feeble.

Rough hands dragged her away from the heat, and as she struggled, a fireman assisted her out of the blanket. He offered his hand and helped her to her feet.

"Ma'am." He tried to place an oxygen mask over her, but she pushed it away.

"Beck. Where is he?"

"Who?"

"The man who saved my life. He got me out of there."

The fireman shook his head. "I don't know. Someone had to have brought you out. You were wrapped like a burrito."

"Could he have gone back inside?" Concern overwhelmed her. Where had he gone?

"Is someone else in the house?" the fireman asked.

Water from a hose rained down on the house.

"Not that I know of. I mean, his son is staying somewhere else…"

It hit Katelyn that she didn't know this man in the fireman gear. Maybe he wanted information. Now she was thinking like Beck—completely paranoid and suspicious.

Katelyn scrambled farther away and stared at the house engulfed in flames. Tears streamed down her cheeks.

"Are you okay?" The face asking the question didn't register. Then finally she realized her brother was the one shaking her shoulders. He'd replaced the fireman. "Katelyn, are you okay?"

"No. I mean, yes. But, Beck… He saved me. We think he might have gone back inside."

Apprehension carved deeper lines into Ryan's features, then a scowl formed. "Why would he do that?"

The safe…

But she kept that to herself. Telling Ryan wouldn't help either of them right now. What did any of it matter if Beck went back inside that house and died tonight?

Katelyn dropped to her knees and watched the flames amid the water spilling onto the disintegrating structure. An explosion boomed and light flashed. Ryan dropped to the ground next to her and held her. Together they watched the roof collapse.

The sky flashed, and she thought it was another explosion, but thunder rumbled. Drops of water hit Katelyn's forehead. She looked up, expecting to see a hose flying in the wrong direction.

"It's raining. Yes, it's raining, Katelyn." Ryan pumped his fist. "We haven't had rain in much too long. Thank You, God!"

She covered her eyes. "He saved me, Lord…" *He can't be dead. He just can't be dead.*

Arms gathered her against a broad chest and Katelyn let the rain join her tears.

"Katelyn, it's okay."

That voice. His voice. She pushed back from that chest to look up into Beck's gray eyes, rivulets of rain washing down his face.

She had thought Ryan was comforting her. She glanced around and spotted him now talking to a fireman. She focused back on Beck. "I—I thought you were dead. If you didn't go back into that house, then where did you go?"

He cupped her face and stared into her eyes, oblivious to the rain. The dying fire lit his drenched hair and face. Katelyn didn't care that others watched the two of them. At this moment in time, she only cared about Beck. She held the connection as long as she could. Life could be snatched away in milliseconds, and tragically. Or someone could give their life to save another's.

Katelyn had thought she'd lost Beck.

"I'm sorry I left you, Katelyn." He rubbed his thumb against her cheek. Emotion flared in his warm, searching gaze, which seemed to sweep through her soul. "Firemen had arrived. I knew you were safe. I skirted the houses to watch for myself."

She nodded. "You mean you were looking for the person who deliberately locked us in the basement and set fire to the house."

His lips smiled as a laugh burst from his chest. "Yes."

"You were worried I wouldn't track with you."

He nodded.

"And you wanted to hear me say it first."

He nodded and pressed his forehead against hers. Emotion welled in her heart—but from the near-death experience? From almost losing him? Or should she listen to the alarms going off in her head warning her that Beck Goodwin was eroding her protective walls?

A blaze consumed his home. Firemen doused the flames. Rain drenched them. Neighbors gathered. But none of it mattered. All of the events surrounding him seemed far away and down a long tunnel.

Heart pounding, he kept his head pressed against Katelyn's. Time seemed to stand still as Beck held on to the connection he had with this woman.

I could have lost her tonight.

She meant much more to him than just a hired private investigator. More to him than a neighbor or a close friend. Yes, she was a friend, a good, close friend, like he'd told Ollie. But more than that, Beck and Katelyn were kindred spirits, and more than anything he wanted to know her so much better. Why did he feel such a strong emotional connection with her? Why was he constantly dodging the magnetic attraction to her?

If only he could trust her with his heart. He wished he could get over his inability to trust, but Mia—even if unintentionally—had destroyed that part of him.

Suddenly the world around them crashed through the moment and broke them apart. He grabbed her hand and pulled her even farther away from the sizzling house and down the street where he'd parked. Beck tucked her into his vehicle, where she would be safe and warm. He reached for the door to shut it but she pulled him to her.

"Beck, I forgot to thank you. Thank you for saving my life. For saving us." Her hold on him drew him closer. He found himself millimeters from her face, from her lips that he knew would be supple, and fought the need to have them. He hesitated, wanting to know...

Then she met him halfway, and her soft lips pressed against his mouth. He wrapped his arms around her and savored her warmth, her beauty, both inside and out. She was everything he wanted but couldn't have.

A throat cleared.

Beck slowly released her, but he held her gaze. He was keenly aware her brother stood behind him. When he dropped his arms, she slid all the way into the truck and he closed the door. There. Now she was safe and warm.

He ignored Ryan's glare and jogged around to the other side of the truck. Ryan gripped his arm and whirled Beck to face him. "Where do you think you're going?"

Beck scraped his arm across his face to wipe the rain out of his eyes. "Trying to get warm, that's all. What's your problem?"

"You have a lot to answer for tonight. Your house just burned down. How do you explain that?"

"I can't explain it. Someone will have to in-vestigate," Beck said. No way was he going to offer up his theories only to have them trampled, or be accused of being crazy again.

He could already hear that conversation in his head now.

It would go something like this:

"Why would someone try to kill you?"

"Because they think I'm going to discover what my wife was hiding. That she was a federal agent. Maybe CIA."

"Uh… Huh. And why do you think your wife was a spy?"

"She acted funny. Strange. I saw her with someone."

"Uh… Huh."

"I found a safe. She was hiding her secrets inside."

"Uh… Huh."

No, thank you very much. He'd tried with the police. If he was on the right track, he would find something to validate his suspicions and then the hard part would come—finding whom he could trust with the information to investigate Mia's death.

And right now…

His son. He had to think of Ollie. He had to keep his son safe.

And Katelyn.

Shame engulfed him. She was in this now and he couldn't help but blame himself.

"Believe me, someone is going to investigate." Ryan's tone was threatening.

"Ryan!" Katelyn had exited the truck and stepped between the two of them. "Beck saved my life tonight. He risked his own life to save mine."

"To be fair, we were both going to die," Beck added.

"Do we have to discuss this in the rain?" She shivered and wrapped her arms around herself, glaring at both of them.

Beck and Ryan both instinctively reached for her to wrap their arms around her, but collided. Beck pulled back and Ryan took the protective stance toward his sister.

Katelyn shrugged away. "Will you stop this, Ryan? I'm not a child."

"What were you doing in the house?"

Katelyn's eyes remained on Ryan's. She flinched but didn't glance at Beck, which would telegraph they held a secret between them. He didn't want Ryan asking too many questions.

"Back off, Ryan. The fire chief will investigate and then we'll know something."

He literally took a step back.

"Don't you have a date with your future wife tonight?" Katelyn asked. "Now, I'm cold and tired and shaken." She stepped close to Beck and wrapped her arms around him as if letting

Ryan know they had a thing going, which they didn't, and yet, they did. Beck was getting confused, and he needed to avoid that confusion at all cost. But he understood that she was doing this to push Ryan away from their investigation.

Her brother lifted his hands in surrender and started to walk away, but gave Beck a warning look before he left.

Beck was duly warned—but not because he was afraid of Ryan.

No. He was more afraid of himself and how being with Katelyn affected him.

Still, that came second to keeping them alive so they could discover the truth.

NINE

Katelyn took in the scene and was stunned to see the protectiveness in Beck's eyes—protectiveness equal to her twin brother's. How could that be? She couldn't process it. Beck remained a statue, rain pelting him and dripping off him as if he was stone, while he watched her brother stalking away.

Time to redirect. She grabbed Beck's shoulders and turned him to face her. Turned his attention back to her. "Never mind him. Let's get in your vehicle and out of the rain."

She held his gaze until he seemed to shake off whatever darkness consumed him. "Right," he said. "Let's do that."

He ushered her around to the passenger side and opened the door for her. Not that he needed to, but Beck was a gentleman and Katelyn didn't want to stand in the way of that.

At some point, Beck had shifted from being not just her client, but a man bent on protecting her. Katelyn wasn't sure how she should handle that, but it wasn't like she could turn him down—he'd saved her life back there. And a few minutes ago she'd sent away her brother—her brother, who also wanted to protect her. She shook off the guilt. Ryan had meant well, but she didn't need the stay-away-from-her, big-brother act from him.

And… She hoped as she and Beck dug deeper into this mystery that she wouldn't need her brothers'—all of them—assistance.

Or Tori's. She and Ryan needed their wedding day to go off without a hitch.

Katelyn shuddered. *God, please don't let me be the weak link here. Just…let them get married.* She'd done her part to keep Tori in town so they could have another chance. The last thing she wanted was to be the obstacle in their path.

Beck opened the door, climbed in and slammed it. They were both soaking wet, and even though it was the end of the summer, it was chilly out. He turned on the vehicle and cranked up the heat. Beck reached into the back seat and grabbed a fleece hoodie. "Here, use this."

She shook her head. "No, it's yours. You're cold, too."

He ignored her suggestion and blanketed the hoodie over her. "We need to get out of here. Get somewhere safe. Except—" he shook his head and growled "—I want to get back into what's left of my house to get that safe. I can't believe after all this, we still don't have it or the contents inside."

"You can't go back in."

"Don't you think I know that?" He huffed. "I know I can't go looking around until they're done investigating."

"And not until the embers have cooled." She wanted to reach for him, but that was becoming much too comfortable. Katelyn was getting out of her depth with him. Crossing the lines she'd set. Instead, she wrapped her arms around herself beneath the fleece hoodie he'd thrown over her. "I'm so sorry, Beck. I don't know what else to say or think."

As the heat warmed them, they watched the flow of water from the fire truck hose finally stop, and the flames finally die out. Between the firemen's work and the skies opening up, the dragon had been slayed, and the fire destroyed. Charred remnants, blackened pillars and wet ash was all that remained.

Even the last of the neighbors who'd stayed out in the rain to watch finally returned to their homes.

Katelyn's heart ached at the sight, her emotions reeling from the roller-coaster ride. First fear, then relief, and now pain so deep she couldn't describe it. But they were alive, and for that she was also grateful.

"What am I going to tell Ollie?" The defeat in Beck's voice nearly broke Katelyn.

She made no attempt to answer his question.

If that wasn't enough, in the midst of the tragedy and loss, and the attempt on their lives, the intimate kiss they had shared fought for space in her mind and heart. The emotions had overwhelmed her. Maybe she'd always had a thing for him, deep inside, which had developed from the few times she'd interacted with him in the past.

But the question of her heart—could she love someone like Beck? After the kiss, she knew without a doubt that he was someone she could fall for. He was a good man, but right now they both had serious, life-threatening issues facing them.

But at the end of the day, even if they didn't, all she had to do was picture Tony as she took those pictures for a husband who had hired her to find out who his wife was cheating with, and her stomach would instantly turn.

Reflexively, she leaned closer to the door and away from Beck. She couldn't trust anyone again, so would fight to keep her heart in check.

"Stay here," Beck said. "I'll go check with

the firemen again to make sure it's okay for us to leave."

Katelyn should go, but it was Beck's house and she didn't want to face her brother. She hoped he had gone to his dinner date with Tori. Tomorrow night was the rehearsal dinner, and Katelyn would not ruin that for them. She would not be the reason for interruptions in their wedding plans.

Beck got back in the vehicle. "The rain helped the situation, but the house is still destroyed."

"What did they say?"

"They suspect arson. I could be a suspect. The fact that I was still in the home and saved you is in my favor, though. But they'll have to process through that. Someone will call me as soon as the fire chief has completed his investigation."

"In the meantime, we need to stay somewhere safe, Beck."

"I hope you're not suggesting your house, Katelyn. You've been attacked in your home, and it's only two houses away. I wouldn't consider that safe."

"Then where?" Because if Beck was right and Mia had been with an agency—like the CIA—then whoever they were battling could have resources, and in that case, nowhere was safe. Even staying at a hotel could signal their whereabouts to anyone who knew how to look.

But there was one place...

She snapped her fingers. "I know where we can go. We have a family lake house up by Shasta Lake. No one will be there. Why didn't I think of it before?"

"That's still connected to your family, Katelyn."

"Do you have a better idea? Because right now, I don't." She sighed. "Look, it's safe for now, even if only for a few hours, and will give us a chance to regroup."

Frowning, he subtly shook his head.

"I'm going to grab some dry clothes at my house," she said. "No one is going to bother us there. Too much going on in this neighborhood tonight." Katelyn hesitated, then said, "Oh, I'm sorry. What about you? You need dry clothes, too."

How could she be so insensitive?

Then his right cheek hitched with a dimple. "I've always got extras in the truck. With the climbing, I never know when I'm going to need a change of clothes. Well, that's not true. I usually always need a change of clothes."

"Yeah, well, you're going to need something nice enough to attend a rehearsal dinner tomorrow night for Tori and Ryan's wedding. I can't miss that, and I don't want…"

"Yeah?" He watched her, waiting for her to finish what she was going to say.

She had a feeling he already knew because this was becoming a thing with him—he wanted her to say the words.

"Okay, um… I don't want you to leave my side. And not for the reasons you think."

"What would those be?"

Her throat tightened. What was he going to think about her take on things? He might think it was all twisted up. "I'm protective of you, Beck."

There, she'd said it—only her words were the complete opposite of the truth. She wanted— needed—his protection.

As Beck parked in the driveway of the dark home by the lake, his protective instincts kicked up a thousand notches. He'd hired Katelyn partially under duress, and while she was an ex-cop and had all the skills, she had no idea how protective of her he'd become. He didn't want her putting herself on the line or in harm's way for him. If she hadn't done that to begin with, he would be in this alone.

That's where he should be. In this alone.

That would be safer for her, and safer for

Beck—he felt the connection he had with her growing stronger each moment he was with her, despite his attempt to keep his heart stone-cold.

As he killed the lights on his truck, he turned to Katelyn. "Wait here. I'm going to check the perimeter."

She laughed.

"What's so funny?"

"I was the cop. I still have those skills, believe it or not, so let me do this."

"We'll do it together." He got out and walked toward the two-story home with a rocked front and a blue door. He figured the back was filled with windows for an amazing view of Shasta Lake. The family had some bucks somewhere, or maybe the home had just been in the family for a long time. Laughter echoed across the lake.

Above the evergreens, a few stars could be seen beyond the clouds moving out after having dumped their load on a dry Northern California.

Insect noises filled the night as he and Katelyn crept forward.

They both brandished weapons, and he hoped no one spotted them. Neighbors could misconstrue them as a threat to the homeowners. If the police were called, that could give them away to the assailant from whom they were hiding.

The home breaker. The killer. The arsonist.

His cell phone buzzed in his pocket. Retrieving it, he recognized the caller. "Mom, everything okay?"

"Yes. Ollie wanted to say good-night."

Ollie's voice burst through the cell. He said good-night to his son, his heart aching. He had no idea how he would break the news to Ollie about their home, or to his parents, either. Since they were camping through the weekend, he hoped this would all be resolved and he could tell them before they saw it on TV. He also hoped that the news he gave them would include letting them know the bad guy, Mia's murderer, was behind bars.

He ended the call and jogged to catch up to Katelyn. "I'm not sure this was such a great idea anymore."

"Neither am I, but we're here." She lifted a brick and found a key.

"You live in a family of cops and you guys keep an extra key under a brick?"

Without answering, she unlocked the door, then quickly moved to disarm the security system. At least they had one. He felt a little better.

She flipped on the lights and together they checked the house to determine if it was safe. No security breaches here. No walking into a break-in.

"I'll grab our bags." He plodded out to his truck, images of the fire chasing him. Thoughts of Katelyn in his arms, depending on him for their lives…and all because of that stupid safe.

And here he was, no better off for their efforts. Somehow he had to get his hands on the contents of that safe before someone else did. He couldn't be sure no one else had. And he couldn't be sure the safe was "fire safe," as most claimed.

When he returned, Katelyn was making coffee and grilled-cheese sandwiches. She flipped a blackened sandwich, scrambling to save it, and smiled up at him. Then her focus went back to salvaging the sandwiches. They were charred and he pushed images of his house out of his mind—easy enough, when he looked at her smile.

But he could tell the smile was forced. Her eyes lacked that sparkle, that I'm-every-woman determination that he admired so much. Her smile and the sandwiches were meant to offset the heaviness. They both needed levity. Too much had happened in a very short time.

He dropped their duffel bags on the plush sofa and looked around, admiring the spacious room, wood floors and brick fireplace. Cozy furniture. And beyond those big windows, he knew a big deck looked out over the water. He'd seen it on their perimeter check.

"I told you the place was stocked. I could

have made something else, but this was quick and easy. Someone must have stayed here last weekend. The block of cheese was new and the milk was still good. Bread, too. So I'm making dinner. Oops—" she dropped the hot sandwiches on plates "—that was close. Sure they're a little burnt, but at least you don't have to eat on the floor."

"At least." In that moment, he found her utterly irresistible.

His stomach growled and she laughed.

She set the plates on the counter. Pushed a glass of milk toward him. "At least I know you like milk. I hope the sandwiches will do."

"This is great." He couldn't help his frown.

She arched an eyebrow.

"Sorry. I'm…" Something about sitting here and eating sandwiches felt all wrong. Beck should be doing something, but he couldn't exactly figure out what.

She rushed around to him. "You're in shock, Beck. You lost your home tonight."

"Someone tried to kill you again." He couldn't help himself—all the pressure of the last few days closed in on him from all sides, so he pulled her to him. He drew reassurance from her. He couldn't reconcile his emotions—the frustration that she was involved in this, and how grateful he was that she was involved in this.

He finally released her. "I don't know what came over me. Earlier tonight, I shouldn't have..." *Kissed you.*

"I get it. I shouldn't have, either."

She understood him then. It was uncanny how well she read him.

"Let's eat," she said. "Then you can take the loft upstairs and I'll keep watch."

"Wait a minute. I didn't hire you to protect me. I hired you to help me investigate."

"And so far, you're not letting me do much."

"You have to admit, we haven't exactly had a chance. Someone keeps trying to stop us." He stared at the black-crusted "grilled" cheese.

She scooted onto a stool and inhaled her food, oblivious to the blackened bread. If she could do it, then he could, too, and he finished, then chased it down with milk.

"As I was saying," she said. "Pick a room, I'll keep watch. It doesn't have to be the loft."

"We'll take turns then."

She frowned. "Okay. Arguing with you will just waste time. I'll take the first shift."

"You couldn't wait to get cleaned up and change into something dry and warm, remember?" He winked. "I'll take the first shift."

She'd been in a hurry and hadn't changed at

home when she'd stopped to grab a few things. The small duffel she'd packed in hand, she headed down the hallway. She'd flipped on most of the lights when they'd cleared the home and now went through and turned half of them off. The house remained well-lit.

For a few moments, maybe even for the entire night, Beck could actually catch his breath.

A half an hour later, Katelyn had said goodnight and chosen a bedroom near the living area so she wouldn't be too far in case he needed her.

Beck crept quietly around the home, checking windows again and again.

If he listened hard enough, he could still hear the party going on somewhere across the lake.

He hoped the raucousness was the only reason edginess skated across his nerves.

TEN

Katelyn bolted awake. Darkness surrounded her. No light shining in from under the door. She'd purposefully left on half the lights in the house so she should have seen at least a glimmer.

A chill crept over her that had nothing to do with the temperature. She couldn't see her hand in front of her face. Had Beck turned out all the lights?

She doubted it.

Had the electricity gone off?

Or was the worst-case scenario unfolding for them—had someone deliberately cut the power?

Katelyn hesitated. If she got out of bed, the sound could give her away. On the other hand, staying in bed didn't seem like a good idea, either. Fearing someone could be in the room with her already, she waited and listened, then tensed, ready to flee or pounce as necessary.

Then she heard a subtle breath. Panic spiked

through her. She slowly eased the cover away to make her move.

"Beck?" she whispered.

"Yes." His reply was barely audible.

She sensed when he approached the bed. Heat emanated from his body—all that fat-burning metabolism, she supposed. Katelyn reached for her gun on the side table, then completely escaped the blankets. Beck found her hand and squeezed. She held onto him so they wouldn't get separated in the darkness. The clouds must have covered the moon. Absolutely no light leaked through the windows.

Katelyn bit back her need to ask if Beck had seen or heard something. But his actions should confirm her suspicions—the power had been deliberately shut off.

The attacker had found them here at her family lake house. Followed or tracked them somehow—but he was here with them now *in* the house. She fought the shudder that rippled over her.

Was her would-be killer wearing night-vision goggles so he could see them while they walked around blind?

A thousand thoughts raced through her mind. What had the man after them planned for them? Still gripping her hand, Beck started to head out of the bedroom, but she pulled him back in and quietly shut the door. She tugged him to the far corner of the room near the window and leaned close. "No, Beck. We're walking blind out there. He'll see us before we see him."

"Flashlights?"

"He would follow the light."

"What's your plan then?"

Her voice trembled. "I don't know. We could climb out the window instead of going through the house."

"Someone could be out there watching for our escape. Someone could be out there *and* someone could be in the house." His warm breath fanned her cheeks.

"I'm calling 911."

"Go ahead," he said, "but you didn't wait for the police to arrive before bursting into my home."

"Because they wouldn't get there in time." Katelyn bit her lip. She would call for help but they had to rely on themselves to survive.

"Exactly."

"Then let's go out the window. We'll take our chances outside." She felt her way forward and prayed the moon would come out. "You go first, Beck. I'll have your back if he comes into this bedroom."

"It's a risk either way you look at it. You're going out the window first. Just be quick about it." He quietly opened the window, then removed the screen, which unfortunately creaked.

They both froze.

Three muffled gunshots fired through the door. Katelyn stifled her scream.

Beck and Katelyn returned fire.

"Go, go, go!" he shouted and practically tossed her through the window.

Someone kicked the door open as she fell into the bushes.

Bullets flying, Beck dove through the window and rolled through the bushes. Pain ignited like fire as a branch scraped across his back, arms and legs.

Or had that been bullets? Probably not, or he'd feel much worse if he survived at all.

"Beck! Let's go." Katelyn gripped his arms and pulled him to his feet. He stumbled against her, then found his legs and ran.

"Run!" She spoke in hushed tones, but if there had been anyone outside watching the house for their escape, they were dead. He hoped they'd made the right decision.

They were about to find out.

A sliver of moon had broken through the gathering clouds, exposing them and yet lighting their way. They headed for the shadows in the trees that edged the north side of the house.

Her gun ready to use, Katelyn took the lead— she knew the area and Beck didn't. All that mattered was that they got away from the house and the bullets. But neither did they want to run right into someone else who might be watching and waiting.

So far, their attacker seemed to be working alone. But he doubted that with all that was going on, it was a one-man job.

"Whoa." Gasping for breath, Katelyn skidded to a stop. "The lake. I thought we had a few more yards."

Beck gasped for breath and tugged her behind a tree. The moon reflected off the water and he could see the breadth of Shasta Lake, mountains all around. Lights flickered from houses all along the edges of the lake and in the hills. "And I thought we were headed for the woods, not the lake."

Water lapped and he heard it over and over again in his mind. Remembered diving into the water after Mia's vehicle. He had to think about their current life-and-death situation. Stay away from that part of the nightmare from the past.

"I think we should make that 911 call now," he whispered.

"Yeah, about that. I grabbed my gun. Not my phone."

He inwardly groaned. "I dropped mine in the bushes." Weren't they a promising team?

"Then let's head to a neighbor's house and call."

"And away from the water. The neighbor lives away from the water, right?" He should never have agreed to come to a lake house.

"Wait." She tugged him to the ground. "I see him. He's heading this way. I'm going to sneak around behind him. It doesn't look like he's wearing night-vision goggles so he won't be able to see me if I stay hidden."

"And what are you going to do after you sneak around behind him?"

"Apprehend him."

She made to move away and he gripped her wrist. "Katelyn, you're not a cop anymore."

"I can make a citizen's arrest."

He ground his molars as he forced the words out, hoping she would hear the warning in his tone. "You're not going to get that far. He's... He's a trained assassin." *And you might have been a cop at some point, but that was before and now you're a private investigator who is unprepared to face off with an assassin.* The words were truth, but they might hurt her, so he kept them to himself for the moment.

He pressed her down into the grass. Both of them were flat against the cold wet ground.

Water sloshed near his feet. The man crept around the edges of the yard, his silhouette barely visible. The moon disappeared behind the clouds again. The security light from the nearest neighbor's house was like a distant twinkling star and offered no real illumination other than to reveal the stalking silhouette.

"He's getting closer." Katelyn's whisper was hard to hear. "He'll see us if we try to get away now. But... I have an idea."

He had a feeling he wasn't going to like it.

"We can slowly slide into the water and hide there. We could quietly swim our way to safety."

Water. *God, please, not that.*

"If we're going to do this without him hearing, we have to do it now. Time is running out."

Grass rustled behind Beck, drawing his attention. Katelyn was already sliding toward the water. It sloshed up against his ankle, cold and wet.

Oh. His chest constricted. He couldn't catch his breath. Then, he heard no sound other than the lake water lapping against the shore or the grass, wherever it touched.

Katelyn had been right to submerge herself in the water. Would the assassin think to look for them there? It seemed their only choice, but fear kept him paralyzed. He was an idiot. A real idiot.

He could climb mountains and hang on to rocks hundreds of feet from the ground without ropes or gear, completely free-handed, and he was going to let some dark, black-as-night water scare him?

It wasn't as much fear as it was that terror reigned in the depths. Mia… She'd been alive when he got to her, but she'd drowned before he could get her out of her car. She'd been pinned.

He hadn't told Katelyn that part. She'd been murdered, but Beck had been the one to fail her. To let her die.

No one but him, and God knew the truth. His throat grew dry. Now wasn't the time to panic. The slightest movement drew his attention.

He glanced up and could no longer see the skulking silhouette of their pursuer.

The hair on his neck rose. Instinct kicked in and he rolled. Two muffled gunshots sounded at the same moment bullets pumped into the earth. Bullets meant for him.

Beck dove forward, slamming into the assailant, and knocked the gun from him. The man was lightning-fast and punched Beck, knocking him back, and he splashed into the inky black water. Before he could right himself and pull his head up to breathe again, the man was on him, pushing his torso, his face, into the water that could kill. The water that had killed his wife, in the end.

This wasn't the same man he'd fought in his home, or pulled from attempting to smother Katelyn. This man's body was taut and lean. He was more agile. Beck fought for purchase. Anything. His lungs were on fire. One suck on water and he would be gone.

Ollie… Oliver. His baby. His son… He had to live for Ollie.

Water. Blackness. Death surrounded him. His lungs screamed.

Air rushed from his lungs. His body writhed, fighting for air, but he fought back.

If he breathed he would drown.

ELEVEN

Treading water, Katelyn turned around when she sensed Beck wasn't following and peered at the darkness—where the water met the grassy shore was completely black. She thought they'd been in agreement that slipping into the lake was their next move. But she had thought wrong. Beck had been acting funny about the lake—was he afraid of water? Nah, that couldn't be it.

She'd willed him to follow her out, but instead the thumping sound of bullets that erupted from a suppressor had her swimming back for Beck.

The lake remained choppy and her muscles screamed with the effort to swim back to him. Now closer to the house, she spotted the dark shape of a man. His form and movements told her this man wasn't Beck—it was the assassin. He was in the water and was trying to drown Beck. His arms were thrusting into the water and he rocked, fighting to win.

Beck! Her heart stuttered. She had to draw the man's attention.

"Hey! Hey, you! Over here!" she shouted and gasped for breath as she continued swimming for him. *God, please help me make it in time!*

Her feet touched the bottom and she sloshed closer and lifted her weapon. "Stop, or I'll shoot."

Images accosted her. Tony with a gun to his head. Katelyn should have taken the shot. Tony could have died. Someone else, another officer, had taken the shot because Katelyn had been a coward.

Beck would die…

Katelyn fired a warning shot. "The next shot will be in the center of your chest! Let him go. Raise your hands in the air so I can see them."

Though if the man moved she wasn't sure she would be able to see him, dressed in black, as he was on this dark night.

The man lifted his hands. Beck rose from the water, dragging in breath.

And the attacker dove into the inky black water. She couldn't see him. Katelyn aimed her weapon all around. "Hey! Come back here. You're under arrest!"

Then she spotted his form cutting through the dark lake until finally he made the shore and sprinted away.

How long would it be before he came back?

As much as she hated to admit it, she'd have to deal with him later. He wasn't going to go away into the night never to return. Katelyn splashed through the water, her shoes heavy and weighed down, shoving as fast as she could until she found Beck. She plopped down next to him and grabbed him in a fierce hug. His body shivered and tensed, the anger pulsing through him.

She gasped for breath, as did he. *I could have lost you tonight.* "Let's get you out of the water and somewhere safe. Somewhere dry."

He shook his head. "He's probably searching for his gun. Let's get out of here before he takes us out this time. Your first plan—to swim to safety—was the best. I—I shouldn't have hesitated."

He started swimming, and Katelyn didn't waste time. She followed, but her limbs were already growing tired. The water this time of year wasn't too cold so at least they had that going for them. Katelyn swam behind Beck. She twisted to float on her back and then continued swimming on her back. But her arms ached. She didn't know how much farther she could go.

"Beck," she called. "Beck!"

When he didn't answer her heart rate kicked up. She tried swimming on her belly again.

"You okay?" he asked. She'd thought he'd left her behind.

"No. Let's head for the neighbor's pier. I'm not going to make it farther." Together they swam toward the nearest neighbor's home.

Heading in that direction was a risk. They could run in to their assailant there. The assassin could guess that was their next stop because they couldn't swim farther. She certainly couldn't. Though Beck hadn't wanted to take this route, he was a strong swimmer and could apparently outswim her.

As they approached the pier, she tried to search the yard and the shadows in the trees. A security light offered illumination. Maybe the man had given up for tonight.

Please let it be so. Please let it be so. God, please let him just go away.

She continued to repeat the silent prayer while she focused on keeping her pace and just getting to that pier.

Her family had spent many summers—reunions and spontaneous get-togethers—at their Shasta Lake house. Katelyn loved water sports, and before tonight, had thought herself a decent swimmer. But it had been a while and she was out of shape. Water skiing didn't require her to be able to swim across the lake.

Her muscles grew sore and tired until she had no more strength.

Katelyn slipped beneath the water.

* * *

The pier was a mere twenty yards ahead of them. Only a little bit farther. They were almost there. They were going to make it.

Beck had that weird sense that something was wrong. He paused to listen. The gentle splashing of Katelyn swimming behind him had stopped. He whirled around.

She'd been right there. Now she was nowhere.

"No, God, help me!" He swam quickly to the last place he'd seen her, sucked in a breath and dove for her. Once again, he couldn't see a thing. He waved his arms back and forth and…

There. He felt something. Skin. An arm. A hand? But it disappeared.

Mia's face came into his mind. Her eyes had been filled with fear as he attempted to free her. He'd let her down.

He focused on Katelyn and propelled his body in that direction, diving deeper and waving his hand around until he found purchase, then he gripped a hand.

I've got you, Katelyn. Don't let go.

He had her. He kicked until he surfaced with Katelyn. Beck didn't stop there. He didn't wait to have a conversation or a vote on what they should do next, and instead swam with her toward the pier.

Heart pounding, he gave a few good last kicks. Almost there...

Finally they gripped the pier's edge. Beck pushed Katelyn up, hyperaware that their pursuer could be waiting to take the next shot. But their options were few and the worst-case scenarios— drown or be killed by a bullet—didn't change that.

He joined her on the pier and tugged her to him, but his body had no warmth to give her. Together they rose and carried each other onto the grass and into the yard toward the neighbor's home. More security lights suddenly lit up the entire backyard.

They were an easy target.

Then again, the light chased away the shadows and potential hiding places for the man after them.

At the sliding glass door at the back, Katelyn pounded. A window treatment blocked them from seeing inside the home.

"Help. We need help!" she shouted.

"Are you sure this isn't just a vacation home, empty like yours?" He kept his back to the house, watching their surroundings.

"If it's the same neighbor who's lived here for years, she should be home." Katelyn pounded again. "Mrs. Kowalski, please, it's Katelyn. I need your help."

A gray-haired woman pulled back the curtain and opened the sliding glass door. "Why, Katelyn, what in the world? Come here. Come inside." She urged them in, patting them on the shoulders as they passed. "What's going on?"

"Thank you so much for your help." Long hair soaking wet and body dripping water on the tile, Katelyn stood in the room and hugged herself. "I need to use your phone so we can call the police."

Without more questions, the woman handed Katelyn a landline. Katelyn started to punch in the numbers. "Um... Mrs. Kowalski, there's no dial tone."

Katelyn shared a look with Beck.

"Can I use your cell?" he asked.

Mrs. Kowalski disappeared for a few moments, then returned. She handed her cell phone over to Beck. A crease deepened between her eyebrows. "What's this about?"

Limiting her answers, Katelyn explained the possible danger, while Beck called 911. How he appreciated his neighbor Clara's watchful eyes. The police would already be here by now if any of this was happening in their own neighborhood. Except Clara's watchdog approach wasn't a foolproof protection plan, since his home had been turned to ash.

He kept Dispatch on the line and spoke to Katelyn. "Let's find a safe place to wait in the house until the police get here. I'm concerned if the phone line was cut, the power will be—"

The house went dark.

Mrs. Kowalski yelped.

"It's going to be okay." Beck suspected that Katelyn's words were meant for herself as much as for Mrs. Kowalski. "Do you have a safe room?"

"Are you kidding me?"

"Unfortunately, I'm not."

His eyes adjusted and he realized a small light was shining from a plug in the corner.

Mrs. Kowalski noticed his glance. "In case the power goes out."

"Smart."

"You get her somewhere safe, Katelyn."

He braced himself for her counter-argument, but she said nothing. He figured she probably felt a measure of guilt for bringing the danger to her neighbor's door.

But this was all on Beck, and he would end it.

"We'll head for the closet in the back bedroom," Katelyn said. "I used to hide in there with your kids when we were little."

The woman followed Katelyn as she ushered her away.

Now, Beck needed a weapon. He grabbed a butcher knife from the block.

He would be bringing a knife to a gun party,

as the saying went. His only advantage would be one of surprise.

Beck chose a position in the shadows behind a large leafy plant. Waited. Watched and listened.

He had no idea how long it would take before law enforcement arrived, but a lot of harm could be done in ten seconds or less, so he would not wait for them to save the day. He hadn't waited for them to "save the day" for a year now. Nor had he wanted to involve them now, except this time bullets could be retrieved. There was at least proof that someone was trying to get to him, and now, Katelyn.

Even so, the cogs of an investigation would move much too slowly, and he would continue to retain Katelyn's services to get to the bottom of this.

Red and blue lights flashed in the windows as sirens rang out. They'd come faster than he would have thought, for which he was grateful.

Someone pounded on the door. "Police! Please open the door."

Beck stepped from his hiding place, dropping the knife in the plant, then opened the door.

Ryan Bradley scowled at him.

TWELVE

Katelyn tossed and turned in the comfy bed. She couldn't remember the last time she had been so utterly exhausted. She was in the extra bedroom at Tori's home—the house that had once belonged to Tori's deceased sister, Sarah. After giving their statements in separate rooms at the sheriff's offices in the county seat of Rainey, Beck and Katelyn had been released to go.

They had tried to avoid this scenario—bringing others into the mix—but they'd failed on that count. Still, Katelyn planned to be all about damage control. She and Beck could continue their investigation without giving away too much information.

Tori had insisted that Katelyn spend the night with her, while Ryan had said Beck could stay at his house. At least they had somewhere to go, but she worried about Ryan and Tori's safety. Sheriff's deputies had been assigned to each house to make sure anyone with harmful intent stayed away. Katelyn worried about those deputies, too, though.

Like Beck said, this person was an assassin, though if he'd been at the top of his murderous game, they would already be dead. She was honestly surprised that she and Beck had survived this long.

The very last thing she'd wanted was to pull her family into this and put them in danger. But there had been no choice except to call the police last night…and Ryan hadn't been far. He'd been shadowing them. Following them long enough to know she had chosen to stay at the lake house. Unfortunately he hadn't clued into their more dangerous shadow. But Ryan had remained close and that had saved them, and probably Mrs. Kowalski's home, from a few bullets. Maybe even saved her life.

While she was glad for Ryan's help, she felt bad at the same time. He'd canceled his date with Tori—because of Katelyn. She rubbed her eyes. Now they were all in this and she didn't know how to get them out. She had every intention of following through with her responsibility to Beck, regardless of an active police investigation, and despite the fact that Ryan had asked her to stay out of it.

He wasn't the detective in charge, anyway.

Oh, God, show me what to do. I don't know what to do.

A soft knock came at the door. "Can I come in?" Tori asked.

"Sure." Katelyn started to rise, but then dropped back against the pillow. She so did not want to get up to face this day.

Holding a breakfast tray, Tori entered.

Katelyn propped up on her elbows. "What are you doing? Trying to make me feel guilty?"

Tori sat on the edge of the bed and put down the tray as Katelyn fluffed her pillows and pushed up to a sitting position.

"Of course not." Tori scrunched her face. "You've had a rough go of it." Then her frown deepened. "I'm worried about you."

Katelyn shifted in the bed. She wasn't ready to talk about any of it, so she redirected. "Tori, please. If anything, I should be bringing *you* breakfast in bed. You're getting married soon. Your rehearsal dinner is tonight." The wedding wasn't for another two days, but schedules being what they were, the dinner to practice had to be tonight. "I'm so sorry about everything."

"There's nothing to apologize for, Katelyn. This isn't your fault. Evil happens. Bad guys will always exist. That won't stop just because Ryan and I are getting married."

Katelyn sipped on the orange juice. "Well, I

had hoped you would have a small reprieve—time away from the evil in this world, ya know? At least you need time to put some distance between you and crime investigations." Katelyn released a heavy sigh and stared at the breakfast Tori had made. Pancakes, bacon and eggs. She'd gone out of her way. "I've not only taken on a case, but now it's encroaching into all our lives."

"Yes, it is." Tori scrutinized Katelyn. "I wish you would have told me about this from the start."

Guilt again. Katelyn sent her friend and partner a sheepish glance. "I hope you understand why I kept it from you. I want you and Ryan to focus on your wedding and not worry about me."

"Well, maybe we can resolve this together so that we won't have to worry. I know that you would never retract your agreement with Mr. Goodwin, nor would I ask you to. I understand that you're a witness to the crimes, so even retracting the agreement wouldn't change your involvement in this… Whatever it is." Tori stood, then leaned in to hug Katelyn. "Take your time. You're my maid of honor. We're going to retrieve your dress and accessories from your house today to make sure that it's all safe, and then we head to the spa."

Tori fisted her hands on her hips as if daring Katelyn to refuse a day away from the chaos.

"Hey." Katelyn threw her legs over the bed. "I'm the one who is supposed to be treating *you* to this." Tears threatened. "I had planned—"

"Don't beat yourself up, Katelyn. I know how it is. You're obsessed with your job. You're zeroed in on getting the bad guys. Crime doesn't wait for us to have a spa day." Tori smiled. "You can be real with me, remember? That's why we're so close. That, and well, you're my future sister-in-law. Don't worry about whatever you thought you wanted to do for today. The best-laid plans usually get sidetracked, anyway. We're going to have the best spa day we can, and then if we get a call about something pertaining to Beck Goodwin's case, we'll handle that as it comes. But for now, he's with Ryan, so you don't need to worry."

"That's exactly why I need to worry. You know Ryan and Beck won't be having a spa day together. Ryan will not be treating Beck to anything but glares and lectures."

After a shower, Beck dressed in the clothes that Ryan had grabbed from his own closet and shared with him. Though they were a little tight on Beck, he had just lost everything he owned when his home burned. All the memories—the photographs lining the hallway and in the many albums Mia had kept of family times and Ollie. Any keepsakes she'd kept that he hadn't gone through yet because he had wanted to leave the house as it was when she'd passed. He'd been such a coward not to try harder. Not to face all of this sooner.

But last night when the fire erupted, he'd had the courage to keep them alive. Keeping Katelyn safe had driven him, allowed him to push aside the reality of his painful losses long enough to get them through. But now she was in someone else's hands and the roar of the fire razing his home echoed in his mind. At the moment, he was no longer distracted by the need to survive, so the images accosted him.

He sank onto the edge of the bed. Elbows on his knees, he covered his face. Any moment and dry sobs might rock through him. Who knew, maybe he would shed actual tears.

He had thought himself strong but the mystery behind Mia's death, the search for answers, was more brutal than he could have imagined. Somehow he had to pull himself together. He was responsible for starting this search for the truth, which in turn had disturbed the dragon's lair. Beck would not be denied the truth and he would see this through. It had cost him Mia and now his home. What more would it cost him?

The floor creaked, which made him pull his thoughts to the present. The last place he wanted to be at the moment was Ryan Bradley's home. The man knocked on the door once, then opened it.

Arms crossed, he stood in the doorway. "You look the worse for wear."

Beck huffed, but remained where he sat. He hadn't mustered the energy to face off with Katelyn's brother, who was also a detective. He needed the man on his side, at least, at some point.

Finally, Beck rose to look Katelyn's twin brother in the eyes. Ryan was concerned about his sister and Beck couldn't fault him for that. "Look, I appreciate you letting me stay in your home last night." More like insisted that Beck stay, and since he had nowhere else to go, especially since he needed to keep his connection with Katelyn, he had agreed. "But I should get going now."

"Where would you even go?"

"What does that matter to you?"

"It matters because you're in danger and you dragged my sister into this. As much as I don't want to admit it, I think she might have a thing for you. Even if she didn't, I can't let something happen to you. So unless you have a good, safe place to go, you can just stay here at my house."

Beck had been afraid the man would say that. Ryan didn't have a lawful right to keep him here in his home, but he wasn't using that angle. He was using Katelyn. Beck would have done the same thing. He *was* doing the same thing, as it were.

"Fine. But I need to do something. I can't just sit around. It's a waste of time." Beck started doing his incessant pacing in the small room. He hated it was here rather than in his own kitchen. The kitchen where he made Ollie's Mickey Mouse pancakes every Saturday morning. The kitchen where he and Mia had spent evenings cooking together—Beck had enjoyed letting Mia teach him how to cook. The living room where Ollie had taken his first steps. And on and on. The memories could crush him.

Ryan cleared his throat. "I promise, this won't be a waste of time."

Beck allowed Ryan's voice to bring him back to the present. He needed to live in this moment and not the past. Later he could think about what he'd lost, but he still had Ollie to protect, as well as others.

"Aren't you getting married today or something?"

Ryan smirked. "In two days. Tonight's the rehearsal dinner. Katelyn is the maid of honor. She is going to be at that dinner tonight. Tori is going to see to it. And I'm going to make sure you're there, too."

"Me? What have I got to do with it?" Though Katelyn had insisted that he attend with her. That was before they'd been separated, like children.

"Look, just work with me here, okay? I don't want to have to worry about my sister or my future wife. If you're there, then I won't have to worry."

Beck thought about throwing out "What's in it for me?" but that wouldn't be wise. He wanted Katelyn to be safe, too. He and Ryan were on the same team.

"Aren't you concerned for Katelyn's safety if I'm there? Or even if I'm not? Someone tried to kill her and not just once."

"We have law enforcement on the houses, and they'll be at the dinner *and* the wedding."

"Can you afford that kind of contingency? Don't you have a big county to cover?"

"As far as I know, you're the only two people who have allegedly been attacked."

"There you go, using police speak again." And it sounded an awful lot like the past, when he couldn't convince them his wife had been murdered.

"So please humor us all and come to the rehearsal." Ryan dipped his chin, leveling his gaze on Beck. "For Katelyn's sake."

There he was using Katelyn again, knowing full well that Beck would comply. Beck shouldn't go. He should get back to the house and try to get to the safe before someone beat him to it. Maybe lead the assassin away from Katelyn, but the truth was, he couldn't do this alone.

"And just so you know," Ryan said, "Katelyn has two more brothers. Also in law enforcement. Reece is a special agent with the National Park Services ISB. The Investigative Services Branch. Then there's Ben, who was military police and is now a US Marshal."

"Is that a threat?"

"No. The point is that we have ample protection." Then Ryan smirked. "But you can take it as a threat if you want. Be ready to go in fifteen minutes."

"Where are we going?"

"I thought I'd make it my business to torture you today." Ryan sighed. "That wasn't fair. Sorry. You seem to think that's what I want, but honestly, I just want to help. Your house burned down. You need clothes and…much more."

Ryan sounded sincere, like he wanted to help Beck, but he was getting married. Starting a life with the woman he loved. Beck wouldn't get in the way of that. He wouldn't cause more trouble than he already had, even if indirectly.

"And it sounds like I need a decent suit to wear tonight."

THIRTEEN

Since Ryan had insisted a deputy accompany them today, Katelyn would try and relax a little. After all, it was broad daylight. They should be relatively safe. She watched Tori peel the cucumbers off her eyes.

Tori turned to stare at Katelyn, a funny look on her face. "I always wondered what this kind of pampering felt like. I decided that I'd try it because, hey, I'm getting married."

"Yeah. It was never my thing, either." Katelyn laughed. "Oh, I'm sorry. Were you saying it *is* your thing now and I misunderstood?"

"You didn't misunderstand." Tori snorted a laugh. "So… You can't stop thinking about him, can you?"

Tori sat up and began wiping the mud from her face.

"What are you talking about?" Katelyn rubbed a big white towel over her own face, though maybe she was supposed to use a wipe or something. Oops. She hoped she didn't mess up their towels. But what did she know? Nothing. Nada.

"Beck Goodwin. I'm talking about your neighbor. He's a looker. Kindhearted. Athletic. Seems to care about you."

Katelyn dropped the towel. "My only concern about him is regarding the case he hired me to help him investigate. I'm concerned that he has an assassin after him."

"I don't think this guy is an assassin."

Katelyn followed Tori to the showers and dressing rooms. "Why do you say that?"

"I mean, if he were actually an 'assassin'—" she used finger quotes "—you'd be dead, wouldn't you?"

"What do you take me for? I'm an ex-cop. And Beck—"

"Beck is what? He isn't trained as a cop. He wasn't military, was he? So how have you guys escaped this threat going on, what, four attempts now? I'm not buying that this man is a trained assassin."

"Well, I don't need you to buy it, Tori. I need you to stop thinking about my case and focus on my brother, okay?"

Tori approached Katelyn. "I want to focus on Ryan. It's my dream to think only of him, but you're in trouble."

"What are you going to do? Take me on your honeymoon with you?"

Katelyn's cell rang, jarring her. She snatched it from the counter without even glancing at the image. "Katelyn speaking."

"We heard from the fire chief," Ryan said. "We're good to go in and look for Beck's safe. And yes, he told me about it. I'm giving you a courtesy call on this. Detective Manning is still working it."

"Is—is—?"

"Yes. Beck's with me. He'll be there. Tell Tori I'll stop by and pick you up on the way to the house. She doesn't need to be involved."

Tori snatched the cell from her. "If you're going to be there, I'll be there."

Katelyn backed off. This had turned into her worst-case scenario. Her involvement was getting in the way of their wedding. She snatched back the cell.

"Ryan, let Manning handle this. You and Tori focus on each other. I don't want to be the reason you aren't, and I'll never forgive you if you make me that reason." Frowning, she was unsure if she was making any sense.

"Don't worry, sis. Both Ben and Reece will be here this afternoon. Tell Tori I love her, and I'll see her tonight."

He ended the call.

Katelyn looked at Tori. "Not sure if you heard that, but Ben and Reece will be here this afternoon and Ryan is handing me off to Manning and my other brothers, for lack of a better way to put it. He said he will see you tonight and that he loves you."

Tori twisted her lips into an uncharacteristic pout.

What would it be like to hear those words from someone she loved, and to truly be able to trust them? Would Katelyn ever know?

"Let's get back to your house so I can be ready. I promise I'll be back in time to help you dress for the rehearsal dinner. It'll be all right, Tori. I'll be all right."

Two hours later, Katelyn climbed from Ryan's county vehicle. Reece and Ben had been running late, so Ryan hadn't yet handed her off as promised, but Tori had been kept in the dark on that point. Just as well. "You shouldn't be working this week. You should take the entire week off." She was beginning to sound like a broken record and her brother wasn't listening.

He slid his gaze to her and said nothing. Just walked across the lawn to the charred remains, where Detective Manning and Beck waited on the edge of the burned-down home.

At the sight of Beck her heart pinged around inside. His build seemed to dwarf the detective's, but his demeanor revealed his anguish. He appeared defeated. Her heart ached at the sight. She wanted to rush up to him and hug him, but not with all the professionals looking on. She was supposed to be a professional, too, after all. He'd hired her as a private investigator, and look where that had taken them.

"Watch it. There are still a few hot spots. You can recognize them with the spirals of smoke." Detective Manning stood on the southwest corner at the back. "Mr. Goodwin tells me the safe should be right here."

"This is where I remember it," she said.

"Oh, so you saw it, too."

"Yes. I tried to break into it to help Beck."

He gave her a severe look. Yeah, maybe they had been messing with evidence. Actually, they were trying to get evidence enough to convince the police there was even a case.

"The house collapsed inward, most of it turned to ash. But from here, we can see down into the basement. We can see what's left of that wall." Manning marched around to the opposite side and everyone followed. "We'll get our guys in here to dig around, but…"

The detective hopped down.

"Watch out!" Ryan yelled.

A board snapped with Manning's weight. He was an older detective and an ornery know-it-all, and thought he knew what he was doing. Maybe he did. Katelyn was too exhausted to argue. She wanted to talk about all of it with Beck.

Alone.

Her mind was reeling with chaotic thoughts about everything that had happened, and her heart ached for reasons that went beyond explanation.

Manning used a rod he'd lifted to move stuff around. Very scientific and evidence-preserving of him.

"Nothing. See? Here's the spot you say it should be."

Ryan crouched as he looked down into the exposed basement. "You can see the cutout in the wall where a safe would fit. The hole is blackened, but it's still there and… Empty."

Katelyn's heart pounded in her ears. She glanced to Beck.

His tanned skin seemed pale. "Someone took it in the night. Someone took it because you weren't watching the house. I told you to watch the house. I told you that someone was after that safe. And just like always, you didn't believe me."

"Look. I believe you," Manning said.

Ryan nodded. "We believe you, Goodwin."

"It's too late," Beck said. "The answers were

in that safe. Your so-called help only made things worse."

"Beck," Katelyn said through gently clenched teeth. She approached him slowly. Per usual, he was a tiger waiting to pounce. She'd had that feeling before about him. He was wound too tight, and anger was getting the best of him. She peered up at his gray eyes, grown dark now, and saw the storm brewing there.

She spoke in low tones, so only he could hear her.

"I gave you the benefit of the doubt from the start. Now I need you to believe me. Don't worry. I'm here and we'll find the answers. But you can't take it out on these guys. You need them on your side." Katelyn held his gaze, pleading with him to dial down the tension, as if she had the power over him to control that.

"Well, now that they have what they want," Manning said, "maybe that means you're safe."

Katelyn still held Beck's gaze, and she saw in his eyes what she also suspected—they weren't safe now and depending on the contents of that safe, they could possibly be in even more danger.

That evening, Beck waited with Ryan at a fancy Italian restaurant in a private room where the rehearsal dinner was being held. Ryan and his family had participated in the wedding rehearsal earlier that evening. Upset over the loss of the safe, Beck had begged off and fortunately Ryan had acquiesced to his need for some alone time. He'd stayed at Ryan's house, a deputy guarding the place, while the wedding practice ensued. But Ryan had returned in an hour to get Beck for the dinner. Ryan insisted Beck couldn't miss that—Katelyn was expecting him there.

So here he sat, waiting for the rest of the wedding party to arrive. Apparently Tori had also wanted to change before dinner.

So he waited next to her detective groom-to-be, wondering how he found himself in this situation. Beck had once thought that if only the police would believe him and take him seriously, then his circumstances would greatly improve. Now they believed him, and that belief had changed nothing. He still had no answers, and Katelyn was still in danger.

Who was he kidding? He was still in danger, too.

A deputy had taken Tori and Katelyn home, and then would be escorting them to the restaurant. That let Beck know that Ryan didn't go along with his detective coworker's assessment that Katelyn was out of danger now that the safe had been taken. Ryan wouldn't leave his bride-to-be and sister unprotected.

Smart man.

Any other time, Beck thought he and Ryan could have been friends, but the man still didn't trust Beck. Two men approached the table where Ryan and Beck waited, and Ryan introduced him to his and Katelyn's brothers, Reece and Ben. Both sharp-looking men. Just how much of what was going on had Ryan shared with his brothers? By the expressions on their faces, everything.

He could tell by the looks they gave him that neither approved of Beck's presence in Katelyn's life. How did she operate successfully as a private investigator when they were in her business like this?

The next thing Beck knew the room began filling with way too many people—members of both families. Tori Peterson's parents, along with the Bradley family. Katelyn's parents, too. Beck tried to shove away the idea that he was "meeting the parents" of a woman for whom he had long-term intentions. Thankfully he didn't get the sense from Katelyn's parents they had been clued in to the goings-on with his case and the potential for danger. The law-enforcement presence could even be here without the danger Beck brought to the proverbial table.

Suddenly Ryan's guarded eyes shimmered and a smile erupted. His brothers' faces shined, too.

That could only mean one thing—the ladies had arrived.

Beck instinctively knew that he would *react* to seeing Katelyn; seeing her all dressed up could most definitely heighten his awareness. He braced himself and turned.

He contained what should have been an audible gasp. She was already beautiful in every way, and he had never seen her dressed in her Sunday best. In this case, rehearsal-dinner best.

Ryan approached Tori to kiss her, and Beck wanted, more than anything, to also approach Katelyn, who stood behind Tori. Katelyn wore a flattering turquoise dress that emphasized her amazing blue-green almond-shaped eyes. He thought he'd prepared himself to see her like this—her gorgeous hair up in a messy bun, exposing her long delicate neck, some wisps of dark hair hanging down to frame her lovely face—but he hadn't realized the strong effect seeing her all soft and feminine would have on him. Katelyn was all woman, and he'd known that from the beginning. Now he knew it in a deep and painful way.

He approached her without realizing that he had, and this close, he now saw that she was

wearing a light sheen of makeup that accentu-
ated her eyes and lips.

Those lips that he'd kissed when he shouldn't
have.

Those lips he wanted to kiss even now.

Someone bumped his shoulder, and still he
couldn't move away. Reece leaned in. "Pull
yourself together, man."

Right. He smiled at Katelyn and closed the
short distance between them, floating as if she
walked on air. Yeah. He definitely needed to
pull himself together. She drew up next to him
as everyone found their assigned seats—Beck
had been a last-minute addition, but he was taking the place of someone who had to cancel.

"You look beautiful," he said. The compli-
ment came from somewhere deep in his heart,
and he tapped down the rising emotions.

"You don't look so bad yourself." She winked.
"That one of Ryan's suits?"

"Nah. He took me to get it today. It needs
some tailoring, but it'll do for tonight."

Her lips parted as though she was speechless.

"Hey, you two," someone teased and others
chuckled. "Sit down so we can focus on the *engaged* couple here."

Heat ignited his neck and cheeks, and he
found his seat next to her, avoiding the curi-

ous looks of Katelyn's family. They all had the wrong idea, no doubt there.

He listened to small talk and engaged in it, but was still in a daze, as if he was floating outside of his body and not sitting next to Katelyn at all. His heart rate had kicked up, just sitting next to her. He never thought anyone could make him feel this way again, after Mia died. He definitely didn't want to feel this way again after what he'd gone through with Mia. Her lies, his inability to protect her when it became clear she was in trouble and in danger, and she hadn't wanted to lie to him. He wanted to believe that about her—and that's one more reason it was so important to learn the truth about what happened. He needed to prove that she wanted to share the truth with him, but she had been killed.

If he could do that, then maybe he could be free to love again.

But not yet.

Not yet.

"Where are you, Beck? You seem a million miles from here." Katelyn's voice was soft and her warm breath fanned his skin.

He glanced at her, knowing he couldn't tell her where his thoughts had gone. Fortunately, Ryan's best man, his oldest brother, Reece, drew

everyone's attention by clinking his glass, interrupting Beck's attempt at hiding from Katelyn
his desperate need to be away from her.

FOURTEEN

Reece concluded his toast, then dessert was served. Katelyn remained hyperaware of big, strong rock-climbing Beck sitting next to her in a suit and tie. Her heart had jumped to her throat the moment she'd seen him. Why had she insisted he come to this dinner? Why had Ryan taken him shopping to get a suit? That electricity that sparked when they touched seemed to be buzzing between them and they weren't even touching now. She wasn't rubbing shoulders with him or bumping him and yet the sensation was there. She could almost forget the whole reason why he was there to begin with. She could almost forget their business together. The danger they were in.

That Beck Goodwin was here at the rehearsal dinner was all kinds of strange to begin with. But she had wanted him at her side until the danger was over. She was more protective of

Beck than she had a right to be. His safety was much more to her than simply business.

His safety had become personal. Deeply personal.

Gritting her teeth, Katelyn focused on the variety of desserts served. She had chosen the black-tie cheesecake, but maybe the caramel apple pie would have been good, too. She plastered on a beaming smile. She truly was happy for her brother and Tori, and wished this Beck Goodwin business had happened at another time.

With another private investigator.

Next to her, the timbre of Beck's chuckle vibrated through her. In her peripheral vision she caught his chiseled profile—the kind of profile that was carved into stone statues in some Mediterranean countries. Oddly enough, it wasn't his good looks that drew her to him, but his kindness. That tough, lean and muscular frame housed a sensitive and caring man. Who could resist that?

Until she met Beck, her plan to avoid emotional entanglements had worked perfectly.

All she'd ever had to do was think about Tony's betrayal.

In a matter of a couple of days with Beck, she was already becoming willing to let go of what happened before, so she could forge a new future.

But she wasn't there yet, so there was still hope that she could keep her resolve of never trusting a man with her heart. She hoped they would finish up their investigation and Beck could get back to his life and Ollie—which would include finding a new home somewhere, she was sure—and she could get back to hers.

Friends and family began rising from their chairs, and that signaled to Katelyn the rehearsal dinner was finally over.

She hugged Tori. "I'm so happy for the two of you."

Tori's face beamed with love for Ryan. "You were the one to make this possible."

"What do you mean?"

"Don't think for a minute I didn't see through your scheme to get me to stay here."

"You knew?"

"I just never said anything. But now that it's really going to happen, I owe you a debt of gratitude." Tori winked. "And I'm warning you to be careful with the man for whom you seem so captivated."

Katelyn knew she appeared stunned to Tori. She had hoped she kept her emotions in check; after all, she'd worked hard on that all evening.

"Oh, I'm so sorry, Tori. I hope I didn't come across as, um... What's the word?"

"Preoccupied." Tori laughed. "It's okay. Believe me, my thoughts were on Ryan most of the evening. But a person would have to be on another planet to miss the static charges flying between you and Beck. I just don't want to see you hurt—physically, because of the danger. Or...emotionally."

Katelyn hugged her friend again. "I'll be careful. I promise."

Ryan interrupted Katelyn and took Tori's hand. "Mind if I get a few minutes with Tori before you two head home?"

Katelyn nodded. "Of course. Go ahead."

Beck sidled next to her. He held her gaze, then quickly looked away. What was that about? Unfortunately, she thought she knew—this atmosphere was all kinds of awkward for the two of them.

"Well, what next?" he finally asked. "The safe is gone and now we have nothing. No leads."

Her purse vibrated. Katelyn opened the small black special-occasions purse and found her cell. A couple of text messages had come through from Clara. "Oh, we've got something all right. Clara texted me. She got the license plate of a stranger's vehicle on the street early this morning."

"Why didn't she call the police first?"

"Clara has been in the habit of telling me first for a while now. She has a history of—"

"Being a nosy neighbor. I get it. But what do we do with that information?"

"We're going to run the plates and find out who was sitting near your house. Maybe there is a connection."

"The police are involved in this now, though, so isn't this *their* investigation?"

"Yes and no. I'm still your contracted private investigator and I'm working the case, too. I'll tell Clara to be sure and let Detective Manning know about the suspicious vehicle tomorrow, and then I will also instruct her to go stay with her sister in Spokane," she said. "But I'm not going to wait on Clara or the detective. Now, I need to figure out how to tell Tori that I won't be staying with her tonight."

"I don't think you should go home yet. I'm not so sure you're out of danger."

"Who said anything about going home? After we change, we're going to the office and we're going to find who that car belongs to. It might not be the arsonist, then again, we could find ourselves on a stakeout. If this is our man, I'll call for backup." *As if I'm a cop.* Letting go of her training had been more difficult than she would have thought. Still, if this lead panned out, the cops would make the arrest.

Beck's frustrated demeanor shifted, and half his cheek lifted in a grin as admiration swelled in his eyes.

Oh, Katelyn could get used to that. And that was exactly why she had to wrap up this investigation and get far from Beck Goodwin.

Beck climbed into his truck and waited for Katelyn. She rushed out of the Peterson Bradley Investigations office, then hopped into the passenger side.

"I'll just punch the address into your GPS and we're good to go."

Katelyn had informed Tori she was going to stay at her own home, and she believed she was no longer in danger. Still, Ryan had assigned a deputy outside her house. In the meantime, Beck had thanked Ryan for his hospitality, and for taking him to get new clothes and a suit, but he had a son and family to check on at a campground. That was true, and he did call and check on them. He'd changed out of the suit, and with his new freedom, he planned to see this through with Katelyn's help.

God, please let us finish this tonight. Find out what we need to know tonight.

Katelyn had then snuck out of her own house

and joined him in his truck, which was parked the next street over. While the police were actively investigating the shooting at her family lake house, the house fire and the stolen safe, they wouldn't move as fast as he and Katelyn could.

He had the distinct impression that even though the safe was gone, he and Katelyn were still in lethal danger. Would they always be looking over their shoulders? They had to get to the man and the safe he had stolen before it was too late—which it could very well be already.

GPS directed him and he found himself steering out of town along a stretch of lonely country road, and then finally up a winding mountain road.

Katelyn peered at her tablet—the light as a bit of distraction as he drove in the dark. Finally, she said, "This guy's name is Curtis Hunley."

"And you don't think the vehicle is stolen? Wouldn't a guy committing a crime use a stolen vehicle?"

"In the movies, sure, but most of the time the license-plate number leads us directly to the criminal."

"Regular everyday stupid criminals, you mean."

"There is that aspect. If the people behind Mia's death and the attacks on us are related to some sort of agency, say the CIA, that isn't typical, and we could be looking at a stolen vehicle. Then again, you and I weren't staying there—obviously your house was burned down—so maybe the arsonist took a risk and used his own vehicle."

"I'll guess we'll find out soon enough."

"I thought it best to head to the address. Knowing if he had a criminal background could also tell us something, but running a complete background check would take time we might not have."

"I agree. I think getting a look at him is a good start."

"Right. It will tell if he was the man to break into your house to begin with. The man who tried to smother me."

"When I fought with the guy at the lake house, I got the sense he was a different guy. He wasn't as broad-shouldered or bulky. He was lithe and agile. Also, he carried a gun with a suppressor. A different breed of killer altogether."

"So we're dealing with at least two people."

"Probably more." Beck released a heavy sigh. Was he doing the right thing by keeping her involved? After tonight, if this didn't pan out, he would release her of any obligation to this case. He would fire her.

He'd been selfish to keep her working with him. He'd used the excuse that she had threatened to investigate, anyway. While that could potentially be true, he would bring her brothers in on it to make sure she was occupied elsewhere.

With the thoughts, guilt infused him to his deepest core. If anything happened to Katelyn, how could he live with himself?

But he had to think of Ollie, and since he had opened this door by finding the safe, he couldn't stop now.

"Even if he's not the man we fought with on three occasions now, watching his activities could tell us something. That's why I wanted to do this stakeout before Detective Manning scared the guy off with a visit to his home to ask questions."

"Makes sense to me."

GPS let them know their destination was coming up on the right.

"Keep driving," Katelyn said. "We don't want to make the same mistake they did and park anywhere on the street where they might spot us. We'll hike in and hide in the trees. I've got a couple of pair of binoculars and a good private-investigator, high-quality camera." She held it up for effect. "Plus, we have our weapons."

Beck turned off the GPS so he wouldn't have

to hear the voice repeatedly rerouting him. Then he steered around in the mountain neighborhood and parked one street over. "Our target might not see our vehicle, but someone could see us walking down the street."

"Everything is packed in a hiking back-pack. This is mountain country. I doubt any-one will think twice about us. But we'll keep to the shadows without acting like we're hiding." She glanced up at him. "You can do that, can't you? Act normal at the same time you're trying to be invisible?"

He winked. "I'll follow your example. Lead on."

Katelyn strapped on the backpack, then handed one to him. "We need to both be hikers."

"In the middle of the night."

She shrugged. "We had a rough day today. Got lost and we're just getting back."

Katelyn looked like a hiker in the hiking pants and shirt, backpack and a camera hang-ing across her body. For a moment, he allowed himself to picture her in the turquoise dress from earlier this evening. She had since wiped off the makeup yet appeared equally beautiful.

God, please let us find the men responsible for murder and attempted murder tonight. Let it be over tonight.

Because he couldn't stand this sensation

churning in his gut and growing stronger by the hour—he had a feeling they were walking toward certain death.

FIFTEEN

The heavily wooded neighborhood worked in their favor as they kept to the shadows. No dogs barked, which was also good. No one would be alerted to look out the window and spot two strangers lurking in the dark.

Though this was risky and dangerous, a thrill shot through her. When she'd been a cop, her true dream had been to eventually work for the FBI and maybe even work undercover. But she'd failed so royally at her job that she'd had to let go of that dream.

Was Katelyn putting both their lives at risk by insisting they conduct a stakeout on what could be a dangerous assassin—or two or three—hired by some nebulous government agency to keep Mia's secrets? Even thinking that way sounded utterly ridiculous. And that's exactly why they were on their own tonight.

She approached a wide pine tree and dropped her pack. "We'll stop here." She kept her voice to a whisper. "With these binoculars, I can look at the house directly ahead and see inside. We'll start with this, and then move if necessary."

Beck said nothing, understanding silence was best, and dropped his pack to the ground. She pulled out a dark blanket and laid it near the base of the tree. At his funny look, she simply shrugged.

Why suffer against the cold wet ground if she didn't have to?

Katelyn handed binoculars to Beck and grabbed her camera. She could get an equally good zoom with the telephoto lens. She peered through at the home. Lights were on, but most of the windows were dark, covered with mini blinds or drapes. However, the kitchen window allowed her to see into the dimly lit home. A small light over the sink had been left on.

Was Mr. Hunley in bed already? Or was he brainstorming with his partners-in-crime?

If he was home, then at some point he would go to the kitchen to dump his coffee mug or get a glass of water or milk. Something. The kitchen was the hub.

A shadow caught her attention.

"Movement," she whispered. "Get your binoculars and look at the kitchen window."

A man stood in plain view, but had his back to the window. Dark hair and a sweater or a hoodie. His body language indicated he was speaking to someone either on the phone or in person. He suddenly turned and focused on the kitchen sink.

Katelyn took pictures. Her pulse skyrocketed. Blood roared in her ears and she could hardly breathe. The sensation of the pillow over her face, blocking her ability to breathe, rammed her.

"It's…"

She tried to suck in air, but her throat constricted.

Beck lowered the camera and gripped her. "You're okay. Breathe, Katelyn, breathe."

She nodded and listened to his words. Drew in a breath. And then another. Slower and longer now. She could do this. She could rise above the stupid panic attacks.

"It was him," she said as she peered through the camera. He had disappeared from the window now. She lowered the camera.

"I saw him," Beck said. "It's the same man who tried to…"

Smother me. Beck had held back probably because he didn't want her to start hyperventilating again.

"Stay here." Beck started to rise. "I'm going to face him and get answers."

"Beck!" She held on to him. He'd have to drag

her. "No, you can't go. Let's watch him a little longer to see what he does before he is questioned. After he is questioned by the police, everything he planned to do will change. We need to know who he is working with. What he did to the safe. I'll have to call this in now, but give me a few more minutes."

Beck shrugged free. "Call it in. Do your job. I'm doing mine and that is finding out the truth."

Wait? What about Ollie? She wanted to ask him, but she knew that ultimately he did this for his son's protection. Mia's past, if that's what this was all about, could come back to haunt them all.

"Hold it right there." The raspy voice came out of nowhere.

And so did the muzzle of a gun at the back of her head.

Beck froze in his tracks. Fear curdled in his gut.

Images of Mia's car crash and her vehicle going over the bridge and plunging into the water—it all slammed into him.

Not again, Lord. Please not again. Please keep Katelyn safe.

Beck slowly turned around to face this new threat. A man held a gun at the back of Katelyn's head, but not too close. She had dropped her weapon. The man's menacing eyes glared at Beck as he directed his next words to him. "Toss the gun. Move too fast or try anything and I'll kill her."

Chances were this jerk would kill her, anyway, if they didn't somehow gain the upper hand. But right now the man with the gun was in charge and used Katelyn for leverage. Beck and Katelyn had to work this right or they would both end up dead.

Slowly, Beck pulled his gun from the holster and stretched out his arm. He let the gun dangle from his fingers.

"I said toss it!"

Beck tossed the weapon off to the side, but not too far, his mind scrambling for a possible way out. Presumably someone would come along and retrieve their weapons later. But not this man. This man remained focused on the two of them.

By his build, Beck suspected he was the man he'd fought with at the lake last night, but he couldn't know for sure.

"Now walk to the house."

Beck turned back toward the house and did as he was told. He couldn't look at Katelyn's face. He didn't want to see the fear there. Or the disappointment. Instead of letting his anger get the best of him so that he'd begun to stalk off toward the house, he should have remained by her side. He should have stayed with her and remained on alert. Beck should have protected her. Then they wouldn't be in this no-way-out situation.

When "free" rock climbing, in which he used no equipment to help him climb, he had to have an idea of the path he should take before he even started because he needed handholds in the rock. Footholds, too. But there had been times he had found himself faced with no way up the mountain, which meant going back down to take another path and trying again. If he failed a pitch, then he could return using the rope, the only equipment, and plan a different route.

Failure wasn't an option in this situation. They would not be allowed to try this again. His mind burst with possible ways up the "mountain" of trouble.

And if he couldn't find a way out of this for them, at the very least, he intended to get answers before he died.

But... Katelyn.

Beck needed to survive this for Ollie and his family, and for Katelyn. But how? Anguish could crush him. Though he had no idea what to do next, he would trust God and take one step at a time. One excruciating breath at a time. Sweat trickled down his back as he strode toward the house looking for a way out, or a distraction to pull away the gunman's attention.

But no such distraction came. Another man opened the back door, his big silhouette filling the doorjamb as light poured from the house.

Hunley?

"Ah. Mr. Goodwin. We meet again."

Beck didn't know what to say to that. Had they been introduced other than to tackle each other? He said nothing as the man moved from the doorway and they were escorted inside the typical home, decorated as if Hunley had a wife. Maybe he did and Hunley's wife was clueless to his nefarious activities, like Beck had been about Mia.

"Have a seat." The gunman waved them toward the chairs around a small kitchen table, so they sat. He'd grabbed their packs and tossed them against the wall.

The safe rested in the middle of the table and had been opened. Beck noticed that Katelyn stared at the contents, which were spread out. Maybe she understood more about what she was seeing than Beck did. He'd have to get a closer look and be allowed time to figure it all out. Time he wouldn't get.

"Now that we're face-to-face," Beck said, "maybe you can tell me what this is all about.

Maybe you can tell me why my wife was murdered."

Hunley smirked. "You're too smart for your own good. That's why you're here. Except on that count, bringing the woman into this was stupid. Now she has to die, too."

Fear flicked across Katelyn's features. The man was right. Beck had been stupid to hire her. Idiot. "Look, you killed Mia. That doesn't mean you have to keep killing. So…what? Was Mia some sort of agent?"

The gunman kept his gun trained on them, while Hunley eased onto a chair opposite the two of them.

Beck was surprised they hadn't been bound and gagged, but that could only mean their lives were about to end. These men wouldn't waste the time and energy to tie them up when they were only going to kill them in mere moments.

His pulse raced and he fought to listen to the man's droning words.

"Yes. Your wife—Michaela—was an agent. In the safe she had stashed her alternative identification documents for her aliases, along with incriminating evidence about someone else. I was hired to retrieve the information and kill her. I had to complete my task before I could get paid. That meant watching and waiting for the moment when someone would find where she had hidden it."

Just like he thought, Beck's discovery of the safe had triggered the attacks.

"I slipped into the house and would have gotten into the safe, in and out, without your knowledge, had you not come home too early and encountered my presence. And still, I might have gotten what I needed if your girlfriend hadn't come to your rescue. But she saw my face. That's when the dominoes began to fall." He huffed a laugh. "I can't believe you've survived this long, even after I hired an assassin to take you down while I went for the safe."

Hunley rose.

And Beck tensed, expecting to die at his hands.

He waved his gun around. "I'm guessing that you found your way here because of my license plate."

Beck didn't respond and neither did Katelyn. If Detective Manning got the information and could make his way there to ask questions in the morning, they didn't want to warn off this man so he would leave, and the truth about their deaths would never come out.

Hunley sat again and fidgeted with his gun. He wanted them to think he wasn't worried, but Beck saw through the man's nervous twitches.

"I had a reason to park my car on that street," Hunley said. "I've maneuvered my way into a woman's life. So if the cops come here, that's what I'll tell them. I decided to drop by to visit my friend. As for you, I can't kill you here." He lifted the backpacks. "But you can die a tragic death in the mountains when you fall."

Beck thought he could hear Katelyn's heart pounding. He hoped Clara hadn't waited until morning to call the detective with the news, after all, and that she would have called immediately. Then again, Detective Manning might not act on it until the morning. He would knock on Hunley's door and be greeted by a surprised man, who would hide that he was a murderer.

The window exploded with gunfire.

Blood splattered and the assassin crashed to the ground. Beck shoved Katelyn down as Hunley grabbed his midsection, then slumped in his chair before falling dead on the kitchen floor.

SIXTEEN

Beck shielded her against the bullets, his body covering her on the floor without weighing on her. Katelyn gasped. Fought for breath. Blood. There was blood all around her. Was that a SWAT team outside, taking down their captors? She should feel relief, except she knew in her gut that it probably wasn't law enforcement that had taken out the two men, and it was likely that she and Beck were next. Whoever shot and killed the men might want to question Katelyn and Beck first, so had left them alive for the moment. But they were not going to wait to meet the killer.

"Move. Let's move." Beck urged them over behind a wall and away from the kitchen window. But was that enough?

Breathing hard, she struggled to speak. "We have no idea if someone could shoot us from any of these other windows. We don't know how many of them are out there."

Before she could change her mind or Beck could drag her in another direction, she darted forward and snatched the contents of the safe, then dashed back around to the wall. Another round of gunfire.

"What are you doing?" He ground out the words through gritted teeth.

"I'm getting us what proof we need. Now let's get out of here before it's too late." The gunman had dropped their backpacks within reach. Remaining behind the wall, she slid her arm forward and snatched at least one of them.

Beck was crawling down the hallway. "Katelyn, come on!"

"We could use what's in the pack." Another gun along with hiking gear to verify their story if needed. She shoved Mia's spy stuff inside the pack and put it on her back, then hurried after Beck.

"How are we going to get out of here without the killer knowing?"

A sound from the kitchen let them know the shooter was coming through the back door.

"Hurry," she whispered urgently. This was déjà vu. They'd been through a similar scenario before.

She unlocked the window and pushed out the screen, then jumped through. Beck followed. There was no time to discuss who would go first. They were working as a team, as if they had practiced for this for many years. Katelyn slipped behind a tree, then watched and waited.

Beck held another gun.

"Where'd you get that?" she whispered.

"It's mine. It was on the ground where I tossed it."

Oh.

She pulled the additional gun from the backpack. When it appeared that they were alone, they kept to the darkest of shadows and moved quietly and quickly through the woods. She remained aware of their surroundings, and thought of the possibility the new assassin had not been working alone. With their two main attackers gone, Katelyn was at her wit's end to know who was after them now.

"Let's not go back on the street, but keep to the trees until we get to your vehicle," she said.

He nodded and together they stealthily jogged, then crossed the street at a point farthest away from a streetlamp. Finally at his vehicle, Beck unlocked the doors, and she tossed in the pack, then got in.

Beck was already in. He started the ignition, then they sped away.

"I hope nobody followed us this time. Or for that matter has planted a bomb in your truck."

"Or a tracker."

"Listen to us," she said. "See, this is why I needed to grab this stuff so we have proof."

"I don't care about proving that I'm not crazy and that my wife was a spy. I only wanted to know the truth about what happened to her. Now we know."

"Only what Hunley told us. There could be more. We still need to look at the contents to see why someone would want this so much. The incriminating evidence and such. There could be more than what he told us."

Katelyn had to report the bodies and she called Detective Manning instead of 911. She didn't want some unprepared patrol unit stumbling in on that or the new assassin. She got Manning's voice mail and explained the events of the night. Hunley was dead in his home along with another man, but there was still an assassin out there. And because of that, she and Beck would remain in hiding. She warned Manning to be careful. Guilt suffused her, but she'd done all she could do. They were so close to finding the truth now, and she and Beck would finally get to see the contents of that safe.

Beck drove in silence for a few minutes, glancing in his rearview mirror almost more than he looked at the road. Then he suddenly swerved from the road and pulled over. "We should stop and make sure there aren't any trackers on us."

They both hopped out, and, using flashlights, looked under the truck, in the wheel wells, every place one might possibly stash a tracker. They found nothing. Fortunately, no one had spotted Beck's truck. The shooter had come for Hunley and his assassin, and hadn't expected to see Katelyn and Beck. Maybe that's why they weren't immediate targets.

"Well, that's as good as we can do," he said. "Let's go."

"Where are we going?"

"Some place we can regroup and look through what we've found. I want to see what was in the safe—like you said, there could be much more than what Hunley told us—and then, and only then, we can turn it over to the authorities."

Katelyn said nothing more and figured Beck needed time to process what he'd learned about his wife tonight. Confirming his suspicions might be the one thing he'd desperately needed.

When he drove up an unpaved mountain road, she decided it was time to break the silence. "Please tell me where you're taking us."

"A friend has an old cabin up this drive. We used to come out here and hang out and climb. I had forgotten about it until tonight when we drove up that road to Hunley's house. Something about it reminded me about this place. Chances are nobody is here, so we should be safe for tonight. We'll have a chance to look at the stuff you grabbed."

He turned onto an even narrower road. Branches scraped the window as the vehicle bobbed with the bumps in the road. Finally, he stopped in front of a dark cabin.

Did it even have electricity?

He shifted toward her. "Thank you for that, by the way. For getting Mia's documents and the contents of that safe."

Their connection had shifted now and she couldn't put her finger on it, but with their lives on their line, repeatedly it seemed, their emotions had been scraped raw.

Katelyn wasn't sure she had a wall left around her heart. Not one single stone. "You're welcome. It was important to you." She swallowed against the tightness building in her throat. "To our investigation."

Beck dug around the rocks in the bushes and couldn't find the key. It had been a while since he and his buddy had met at the cabin. He dragged a hand through his hair.

"No key?" Katelyn crossed her arms.

"No key." This would be embarrassing if he cared about what anyone thought of him.

He marched up the porch and tried the knob. Locked. So he simply kicked in the door. He'd have to fix it later.

Katelyn remained on the porch. "Are you sure your friend still owns this place?"

He shook his head. He wasn't sure about anything anymore. When he flipped the switch, at least the lights came on.

Katelyn brought in the backpack and dropped it on the table, disturbing the dust. Beck opened the fridge and found a few bottles of water. The place was dusty and hadn't been used in a few weeks, but someone could definitely show up. This didn't look like Patrick's style. Except… Wait a minute.

Beck spotted a photograph on the wall. Patrick and a woman. Two young girls. Twins. That made sense. He'd kept the place, but his wife had upgraded the decor.

"I get the feeling we shouldn't get too comfortable here," she said.

"Right. Let's look." Though Beck and Patrick had used this as a getaway, he might not be welcome anymore. He and Katelyn wouldn't stay long.

Katelyn pulled the items from the backpack—passports, papers and documents of various sizes—and spread them on the table like Hunley had.

"Hey, what's this?" She handed an envelope with his name scrawled on the front over to him.

Beck held the envelope and frowned. She'd left him a letter? Mia had suspected this day would come then. He opened it and pulled out the missive written in her handwriting.

Reading the letter to himself, he tried to absorb the information as he held back the sobs. He glanced over to see that Katelyn was examining one of Mia's alias passports. She deserved to know what was in the letter.

So he read it out loud.

My dearest Beck,
If you're reading this it can only mean one thing. That I didn't get the chance to tell you in person. To answer all your questions. I'm sorry I've kept you in the dark for so long, but please know that I only did so because you and Ollie are my life. I love you both so much.

When I met you during the world climbing tour, I was working for the CIA. I was a plant in the group so that I could easily go in and out of certain countries. My main task was to uncover a terrorist plot by a foreign entity. I was able to provide sufficient intel to stop the plot. But by then I was in love with you. I'd had enough and wanted out of the CIA. I thought that since I'd succeeded with my task, that a real life should be my reward.

But my handler, Henry Cooley, had other plans. He wouldn't allow me to leave and threatened my life, if I chose to leave. For a while I secretly worked for them even after we married, but I knew my duplicity was wreaking havoc on our relationship. I also knew I wasn't free to leave with Cooley's threats. Instead of living in fear, of looking over my shoulder, I extracted incriminating evidence against him and used it as leverage to gain my freedom. If you're reading this letter, then you have also gotten into the safe. The evidence is with this letter. Please take it to a man who goes by the name Barr. You'll find his contact information is all there, too. My plan was to deliver the information to Barr myself, after I told you the truth. In case something happened to me, I wanted you to know. He is the only person I could trust that wouldn't throw me under the bus when facing off with Cooley. I've been searching for someone trustworthy for much too long and finally found Barr. Maybe I took too long.

If Barr can't be reached, then I advise you to run and never look back. Go underground and never admit to anything. They have eyes and ears everywhere.

You and Ollie build a new life far from here. I've included new IDs for you and Ollie, Mimi and Pops, too.

I loved you with all that was in me, but now I realize that loving you was selfish of me. You didn't ask for a secret agent wife. You never asked for a wife who was so deep undercover she could never reveal her secrets, or that she and her loved ones would be targeted.

That's what they loved about me. I had no one else.

That was, until I fell in love with you, Beck. You're the strongest person I know and at the same time the gentlest. Please find someone else to love. Someone who will be a good mother to Ollie and wife to you.

A tear dropped on the paper. Beck wiped at his eyes. "So, she was going to tell me that night. She wanted to tell me before she tried to get the information to Barr, but she was killed."

"Oh, Beck," Katelyn whispered as she hugged him.

Beck let the letter drop and turned to hug Katelyn to him. He had no more strength to fight the current running between them, and for the moment he absorbed the comfort she offered.

He finally released her, and cupped her face. His emotions were raw and his guard was down. He should feel completely empty, but emotions he didn't want to unpack filled him when he was with Katelyn.

"I thought finding the contents of the safe, finding the truth, would end this."

She chewed on her lip. "But instead now we're only in deeper."

As if it would help her solve a problem, she shoved her hair on top of her head with both hands, her fingers weaving through the silky mane.

Beck looked through the rest of the documents and found contact information for the Barr person mentioned. He also found fake IDs and passports. Four of them, just like Mia had said in her letter.

What kind of life would it be to run and hide? To always be looking over one's shoulder? He couldn't do that to Ollie or his family.

Katelyn was in this now. He couldn't do this to her.

"We have to get a hold of Barr. Give him everything and pray he can shut Cooley down before he gets to us."

SEVENTEEN

Katelyn shifted on the comfy sofa that someone had purchased with sleeping in mind. Beck had secured the door he'd broken open in order to gain entrance and had also been able to contact his friend and ask permission to use the cabin, but for how long he wasn't exactly sure. How long would it take for their pursuer, whom she assumed was this Cooley guy, to find them?

She had a wedding to attend. She was maid of honor and couldn't miss it.

She wanted to tell her brothers what they had found in the safe, but it was the worst kind of information. Would telling them only get them killed? Would anyone who knew die in an "accident" like Beck's wife? She couldn't live with that guilt. And yet, not going to them seemed like all kinds of wrong.

I don't think the local law can help us or protect you. Katelyn thought back to Beck's words to her when this had all started. It seemed like a lifetime ago. He'd been right in his assessment that what was going on went beyond the locals. The sheriff's office would be hard-pressed to investigate or protect, but likely this was out of their jurisdiction. She hadn't looked at the incriminating information Mia had gathered on Cooley, but suspected it would include federal crimes.

She shivered under the throw blanket. Somehow she had to fight the fear wrapping around her.

"Wake up, sleepyhead." Beck gently shook her.

What? She hadn't thought she would ever fall asleep. She'd been too scared. Her panic attacks had been replaced with nightmares about the man after them kicking down the door like Beck had.

She pushed to sit on the sofa. "You made breakfast? Where did you—?"

"I hiked down to the little store on the corner and bought eggs and bacon. Orange juice, too."

"You what? Don't you think that was too risky?"

"I hiked through the back country. The store clerks are used to seeing all sorts. Hikers. Hunters. You name it. No one else was even there. We need food if we're going to keep going."

"I hope you used cash."

"I did, but I'm going to run out soon. Going to an ATM is out of the question."

She finger-combed her hair. "Yeah. This guy is probably plugged in enough to find us through those cameras." She pushed from the sofa, headed to the table and reached for her cell fully expecting a hundred texts from Detective Manning and her family, as well. Ugh. She dreaded answering all the questions to which she had no answers. Not yet, Manning. Not yet. But then she remembered she had turned off her cell phone so the signal could not be pinged and they couldn't be tracked. Beck had done the same.

"We're not going to run out of money, Beck, because we're going to call Barr this morning. And somehow I need to communicate with my family about what is going on. Communicate in such a way that they are not put in danger."

She slid the chair out at the table and plopped down to the breakfast Beck had made her, hoping she would have control over the threatening tears before she lifted her head. Beck was right. They were burning up energy and brain cells and needed to refuel before they could think clearly.

"Thank you for this. It was thoughtful."

He poured her orange juice and hovered close enough that she thought he might kiss her on the forehead, if not the lips.

"You're welcome, but I wasn't going for thoughtful. I was going for smart." His cheeks dimpled as he sat and dug into his eggs.

She crunched on bacon and guzzled the juice. They ate in silence, each burdened by the fear of what could happen next. After breakfast, Katelyn busied herself washing the dishes in the sink. She'd have to remember to write a thank-you note to Beck's friend when this was all over. She dried off the orange-juice glass. And this *would* all be over and everything would go back to normal.

Who was she kidding? This wasn't going to end well.

The glass slipped from her fingers and shattered on the floor.

The sound jarred Beck away from Mia's letter, which he'd been rereading. He rushed to Katelyn. "You okay?"

"Yeah. The glass slipped from my hands. I'll make sure to replace it. I'm sorry."

She bent to pick up the pieces.

He joined her. "Let me do it."

"I've got it." Her voice was strained.

"No, it's okay," he said. "I should have been cleaning the mess I made as I cooked breakfast."

"You cooked breakfast. I can clean it up." She rose.

Beck stood, too. "Listen to us arguing."

"And look, while we fought over who would clean it up, we've picked it up."

He would sweep later for good measure, but wouldn't bring that up or another discussion might ensue about who would sweep. That Katelyn was upset was easy to see. Her hands trembled slightly. He slipped his palm into hers and weaved their fingers together, then led her to the sofa. She sat and he released her hand to plop on the other end.

"What—what are you doing? We should be calling Barr now that we've had breakfast."

Beck had to work up the courage to get through this day. Part of him wished they could stay here and be safe and warm and dry, and away from the real world. Their real world included being shot at by assassins from the spy world.

"Beck, what's wrong?"

He choked a chuckle.

"Sorry, that was a stupid question."

"No, it's not. I was rereading Mia's letter earlier. I wanted to make sure I understood everything. Or see if there was some nuance that we missed."

"As if being attacked and nearly killed multiple times wasn't enough," she said, "this is all so hard for you."

He steadied his breaths. Slowed his heart. "I was thinking about the past. About when I first met Mia. If I had known that she was working as an agent in that capacity, would I have still married her? I was so young and idealistic, I was sure that love could overcome anything at all. I was a world-class climber. I was getting ready to sign on with major advertising campaigns. Mia was a climber, but she wanted no part of the limelight. I gave it all up to marry her. To be with her."

"Beck, don't do this to yourself. Risk is always out there, even when we fall for people who aren't connected to the spy world and assassins."

He hung his head. "You're right. It's always a risk." He angled his head to look at her. "So what's your story?"

"Pardon me?"

"You're beautiful and strong. I can't believe there isn't someone. You know. A boyfriend. A husband."

"Oh." Her turn to huff a chuckle.

He half expected her to counter with "How do you know?" To which he would have responded with something along the lines of how she'd kissed him. He was relieved her response was far from what he expected.

She curled her legs under her in the corner of the sofa.

She definitely looked snuggle-worthy, and he fought the need to wrap himself around her and join her in that corner. Funny that they were having this conversation as if danger wasn't facing them at every turn. Maybe neither of them was ready for what came next.

He definitely needed to take a moment to evaluate his life and his choices—as if any of that could change the unknown future.

"Well, I was a cop in Shasta. My partner, Tony, and I grew about as close as anyone. We worked well together."

"And?"

"We ended up chasing after a dangerous criminal. It quickly turned into a life-threatening situation when he got the best of Tony and held a gun to his head, using him as a hostage. I had my gun aimed at him, and I should have taken that shot. I hadn't been able to pull the trigger—an essential requirement for the job. Another cop took the shot. The criminal fired, too, and the bullet went through Tony's shoulder. He was seriously injured."

"Sounds to me like no one should have taken the shot."

"There was a moment that I could have shot the guy before he had his weapon on Tony. I let that opportunity pass me. My hesitation could have cost his life." Katelyn paused, then said, "I saw the counselor and worked through whatever fear I had that stopped me, but at night I had nightmares. Panic attacks. It was always about that moment when I should have taken that guy out. That is, until recently. Now my dreams are filled with the new terror."

Beck bit back his comments. He wanted to hear the whole story.

"And Tony? You two were close?"

"He never blamed me. I resigned. What else could I do? Tony came over that night with flowers. He kissed me, and that gave me hope that maybe my resignation, the loss of my dream to be an undercover agent..." She gasped and glanced his way. "FBI—that sort of thing. Not...a spy. Not like..."

"It's okay, Katelyn. Please continue."

"He gave me hope because now that I wasn't with the force, we could date. I thought I'd finally found happiness. I even... I even imagined myself married to Tony. I know that sounds silly."

"Not at all. Most people fall in love and dream of romantic bliss." He pushed back the ache inside at how horribly his dream had ended. He couldn't let himself dream like that again. But he could encourage Katelyn.

"Tony cared and I thought we loved each other. That we were going somewhere. I started working as a PI and moonlighting as security around the area. Banks, the hospital. That sort of thing. Someone hired me to follow his cheating spouse. It's not glamorous work, but that's the kind of thing that takes up most of a private investigator's time, which is so sad."

"I agree." He had a feeling where this was going, and he wished he hadn't asked her to share because she was reliving that past. He could hear the pain in her voice.

"I did the work. Followed the woman. Got the picture. She was cheating on her husband with Tony."

Beck ached for the pain Katelyn had experienced. Though different than what Beck had gone through with Mia, it was no less crushing. He reached for her fingers and gently touched them, bracing himself for the current that ran between them.

Somehow, that current had grown stronger and more dangerous.

EIGHTEEN

Choked with tears, Katelyn's throat almost closed up completely. What was the matter with her? Beck's fingers barely touched hers and she knew exactly what that was about. One small spark between them could ignite the hope of a future with this man, and with that thought, she knew that she was well and truly over Tony.

She absolutely wouldn't cry in front of Beck, at least with respect to Tony. Even though she was over the guy, she wasn't over what he'd done to her and the pain he'd caused her—even the mere memory ignited inside her. Good thing she was talking about Tony because it served as a reminder that she couldn't give her heart away no matter how much she wanted to give it to Beck.

But he wasn't asking for her heart. If anything Beck had been severely emotionally wounded by his wife, so Katelyn could forget about her struggle where Beck was concerned. It didn't matter. She leaned forward and pressed her elbows on her thighs, then rested her chin in her hands. "We're procrastinating, aren't we?"

"You got me. I'm a procrastinator." Beck's arm relaxed across the top of the sofa and his gaze held hers. Emotion welled in his gray irises and the current between them suddenly jumped from him and surged up her arms, around her heart and into her belly.

"Beck…" She breathed out his name, and was certain he heard everything that one word on her lips could mean. Her heart was a traitor.

He rose, breaking the current. "I guess we should contact Barr now. I'll get the information."

Katelyn couldn't get enough oxygen. It was like she was on Everest or someplace where the oxygen was limited.

Breathe in. Breathe out.

This was the same panic that overwhelmed her when she had to shoot to save Tony and failed.

It's going to be okay. It's going to be okay. We're going to get a hold of this Barr guy and he'll take the information and get rid of that guy after us. Then I can go to the wedding tomorrow night, and Beck can go pick up Ollie and go buy a new house.

So much remained to work out, and it was all so complicated.

Beck sat at the table. "Why don't you join me? I'll put him on speakerphone. We can talk through what we have and Mia's instructions. I—I need you. I can't do this alone."

Was Katelyn showing that much weakness that Beck needed to beg? "Of course."

She just hadn't wanted to overstep. This was, admittedly, over her head.

Katelyn slid out a chair and sat at the table. Morning light spilled into the cabin and chased away the shadows and the overwhelming fear of danger, and certain death. She could almost pretend that the last few days had never happened.

But then, she wouldn't have gotten to know Beck Goodwin.

He set his cell on the table and turned it on. That in itself was a risk. "Good thing there's a decent cell signal up here."

Katelyn nodded and stared at the phone, wishing there was another way out of this, but they had to make this call. "Go ahead and call him."

Beck punched in the numbers and hit the speaker button. An answering machine came on. He glanced her way. "Not voice mail, but an old answering machine."

Katelyn shrugged. "Maybe voice mail can be hacked and this is more secure?"

He ended the call.

"What are you doing?" she asked.

"What am I supposed to say into an answering machine? 'Mr. Barr, Mia's dead and we're on the run. People are trying to kill us. Please call me or stop by and see me?'"

"Okay, okay. How about you try the number again."

"What for?"

"Come on. Just one more time."

Beck redialed the number. Together they listened as the phone rang.

"Hello?" A woman answered.

"Uh, hello! Hi, my name is Katelyn—" she knew this would sound better coming from her so had jumped in "—and I need to speak with Barr."

"Why? Who are you?"

"Um… Who am I speaking with?" Moisture bloomed on her palms.

"That's none of your concern. Why are you calling?"

"I'm so sorry, I only feel comfortable speaking to Barr. A friend told me to call if… If I was in trouble."

A sob cracked over the other end of the line. "I'm sorry, but he can't help you. He's dead."

"Dead?" Full-on panic swelled in her chest. "How? When? What happened?"

"It's been a year now. I didn't have the heart to change his number in case… In case someone ever called. But now that someone has, I realize there's nothing I can do. It's time to drop this number."

"No, wait!"

"I'm sorry, there's nothing anyone can do for you if you needed Barr."

"But who are you? Are you sure there's no one else?"

The line went dead.

That fear that kept threatening her, that she kept rising above, now snaked around her throat like a boa constrictor and tightened.

A painful silence filled the cabin with the terror of an unknown future. Beck shoved from the table and paced. Nothing was good when he had to resort to pacing.

A chair squeaked, letting him know that Katelyn had risen, too. "Well, Beck, I think it's clear what we have to do next."

"Yeah, what's that?" He kept his head down and his back to her as he paced. "We're out of road here, Katelyn. I don't know where to go."

"But I do."

He wanted to punch the wall and slammed

his fist forward, stopping millimeters from even touching it. He needed to climb. That's what he needed to do. Climbing would purge every foul thought from his brain. From his soul.

Then once he stood at the top of the mountain, he could see as far as his eyes could see. He could take it all in and he would know what to do.

When Katelyn said nothing more, he stopped moving and lifted his face.

Waiting for him, she studied him.

"Well?" he asked.

"Mia's letter said to run and hide. Pretend that you know nothing. That's what we have to do now."

"You can't be serious."

"Whatever it takes to keep our families safe." Her brilliant blue-green eyes welled with tears.

Beck would give anything—*anything*—if Katelyn hadn't moved in to that house six months ago. If she hadn't come to check on him that night. Then one way or another this could all be over and Katelyn wouldn't be involved.

Beck might be dead, or he might not have the safe, but it would be over.

He took two steps forward and wrapped his arms around her. Held her long and hard. Close and tight. They fit perfectly together—from the way he could feel her heart beating, sense the emotions pouring from her, to the way her head rested just beneath his chin.

Holding her was almost like climbing the mountain and standing on the top. He had a great view of the vistas, and right now he knew what he had to do.

She stepped back and turned away. Her turn to pace. "Mia knew what she was talking about," she said. "She knew more than we know even now. If she told you to run and hide that must mean there's no other way. I'm not saying any of this because I'm scared. Yes, I'm scared, but sometimes a little fear is a good thing. Don't you agree if there was another way she would have said so in that letter? She loved you and Ollie. I know she did. I could feel it in her words."

He raised his hands, gesturing for her to slow down. "Okay, stop. Just stop."

She continued, rushing on with more words to persuade him.

"Will you stop?"

Katelyn whirled. "Well, then, what's your big plan? To pace this room? Huh? What has that ever gotten you?"

She rushed out of the cabin.

Well, that's just great.

He'd let her sit out there a while until she calmed down. Clearly their emotions were running too high. He grabbed some of the juice from the fridge, leaving enough for her to have another glass. He hadn't planned for them to stay even this long.

Okay. It had been long enough. He left the cabin and found Katelyn sitting on the porch. He plopped next to her.

"I just needed some fresh air. I'm sorry about that."

"It's okay. You were right. Pacing doesn't do much. But I need to expend energy. If I can't climb, then I pace."

That elicited a rare laugh, and he loved the sound. Her laugh sounded natural and joined the birdsong. He lifted her hand and weaved his fingers with hers. "I wish that I would have invited you to grill hamburgers when you first moved to the neighborhood."

Her cheeks turned pink. "I would have liked that."

She'd said "would have," so she was tracking with his thoughts on this. They wouldn't have a future together, and even if they survived this, each of them had too much baggage.

"I wish we could have gotten to know each other in the normal fashion."

"You mean...? You mean as in dating?" A smile curled the edges of her lips, but not fully.

"Yeah. Like dating. I wish that I didn't have

this mess for a past, and maybe that Tony hadn't hurt you so much."

Beck released her hand, but he remained close. "Katelyn, you know that running won't solve this. It won't keep your family safe. Our families safe. In fact, it could only put them in more danger. And there's just no way we can pretend we know nothing, or that we left no one behind. There's no way my family is going with me using fake IDs."

She sighed. "You're right. Even if we left, I couldn't just leave without telling my family what's going on. And telling them would put them in danger. It's like my greatest fear is happening no matter what I do. No matter how hard I try to steer clear. I've always been so afraid of putting someone I care about in danger, and that due to my own ineptness. That happened with Tony, but I thought I was past that. And now here I am."

"Your being here is only because you have skills, and because you cared enough to come into my house and chase away a bad guy. You were smart enough to get a look at his face."

She shook her head and looked away. He wasn't making any headway with her. She'd have to process through it on her own.

"But the good news is that I know what to do now." Maybe that would get her attention.

When she raised her eyes to him, admiration lingered there. "I knew you would figure it out."

"We're going to take all this to the highest office in the CIA. Drive or fly across the country. Walk in and hand it over."

She snorted a laugh. "What makes you think you can do that?"

"I have to try. If we have to face off with Mia's handler, this Cooley guy, then so be it, but only if it comes to that."

He didn't tell her about the worst part yet, because she really wasn't going to like it.

She was right. He was a procrastinator.

NINETEEN

They had downed protein bars and straightened up the cabin, then grabbed the backpacks, along with the contents of the safe. Katelyn followed Beck out of the cabin. For a short time, it had been a reprieve and she almost regretted having to leave. But it was already growing late in the afternoon. They needed to get on the road and get out of here. A pang went through her heart.

"Okay, well, then. I'm the maid of honor at Tori and Ryan's wedding. I don't know what I'm going to do. The worst thing I could do is bring danger to the wedding. What if men showed up and started shooting?" She searched Beck's gray eyes for answers, even though she knew he had none. "I guess I have to tell them I can't be there, but I can't tell them why, which will only hurt them."

"Shh." Beck approached, his eyes never leaving hers.

He grabbed her hands and cupped them

against his chest. She felt his heart pounding, slow, steady and strong.

"It's going to be all right. You're going to be okay."

"How can you say that?"

"Just trust me. Now, let's get out of here."

Katelyn climbed into Beck's vehicle and watched as he hammered nails into a board that he'd placed across the door and to the adjoining wall, securing it in place. Beck had apologized about the door and promised to send some cash for the fix. He hiked down the path and then got into the driver's seat, glancing her way before he buckled up.

He was asking her to trust him, but he hadn't exactly laid out his plans.

Katelyn had briefly turned on her phone because they were leaving, anyway. She'd received several texts from Tori and her brothers. Mom, too, to which Katelyn had replied that she was working a case. That was totally true.

Beck steered them down the rough mountain road in silence, which was fine with Katelyn. She prayed silently as she thought of how to tell Tori that she had to miss the wedding. How to tell her brother. What could she possibly say that would make any sense?

Maybe she was losing it, really losing it. She now understood how Beck felt when people thought he was being paranoid. But she had lived through several attempts on her life. Maybe that could make a person lose their grip with reality.

She had been a cop once. She'd been strong enough to take on that role, despite her failure at the end.

Beck steered them into Rainey and Katelyn sat up. "Where are we going? I thought we were driving across the country?"

He said nothing, then finally parked in front of Ryan's home.

"Are you kidding me?" Anger boiled in her gut. "Beck, what are you doing?"

He shifted in his seat. "I'm firing you."

Her mouth opened but no words came out.

"I can't protect you but your family can. You're better off with them. I have to do this alone."

"No fair. I know what you're doing. You're trying to draw the danger to yourself. To lead them away. You're making my decisions for me, too, and I don't appreciate it."

He got out of his vehicle and came around to open the door for her, then gestured for her to get out.

"Please," he said. "I couldn't bear it if something happened to you. You talked about failing on your job. Well, I failed before, too. I failed to protect my wife and she's dead now. I can't risk not protecting you. I can't risk failure. Don't make this harder than it already is."

"Beck, you need me." The fury that burned inside was quickly overcome with the ache of failure. She couldn't protect Beck, either. "We worked well together. Didn't I have your back out there? Don't do this."

Regret and fear fought in his gray eyes. She dropped from the seat and stood much too close to him. *I don't want to leave you...* Could he read that in her eyes? Would it make a difference?

"Why do you want to stick around so badly?" His voice sounded husky.

She leaned into him, feeling the draw of everything about him. "I don't know when it happened, but I haven't been in this with you because you hired me, or because we're both running from danger and trying to find answers. I'm here because I care about you...as a friend." Oh, lame. So lame. What a liar.

He acted as if he would reach for her hand but he didn't follow through. "And I care about you, too, Katelyn. That's why you have to stay. I've already contacted your brother to tell him I'm dropping you off."

Katelyn risked a glance at the house and spotted Reece standing at the door.

"Yes, I know this is the day before Ryan's wedding, but no one is more invested in you than your brothers, your family. I have to go now, so I can lead the killer away."

He tugged her forward and she thought he would kiss her, but he stopped short and instead kissed her on the forehead. When he released her, he gripped her shoulders and leveled his gaze on her. "Stay safe, Katelyn. Go live a happy productive life in a career you love. Get married and have kids. Make your dreams come true."

Beck released her and stepped away.

Reece had made his way to the vehicle and he grabbed Katelyn into a big protective brotherly hug. Beck climbed into his vehicle, and without another look at her, drove away.

Excruciating pain throbbed through his chest. But he'd done the right thing. He had no choice. He couldn't be selfish anymore. Beck forced himself to stare at the road ahead of him and not look back at Katelyn. Metaphorically speaking, the road ahead he must travel alone.

He didn't think he meant that much to her, more than that he was a client, but there'd been a brokenness in her features, a sadness in her eyes. Beck had put that there and it crushed him. For not the first time he second-guessed his decision to leave her behind. Earlier, he'd had no choice because of her threat to continue to investigate. But now she had a wedding to attend and three brothers to contend with.

Still, he questioned himself.

Am I doing the right thing? Will she really be safer with them?

Beck had the contents of the safe—the incriminating information from the safe. So someone had to be following him, and not Katelyn. Surrounded by law enforcement, she wouldn't be an easy target.

Beck would be easier. This had to be the right thing to do.

He wanted to see Ollie before he left, but he feared that would only lead Cooley to his son and his camping location. No matter which way he looked at it, there was no good answer. He had a long journey ahead of him, and he wasn't entirely sure how he was going to make it.

Maybe he should convince his family to leave and use the fake IDs, after all.

He swerved and turned onto the street where he lived before his house had been obliterated. One last time he would hike through the ashes, through the memories of the life he'd lived and loved. Remember what he'd once had with Mia. The good and the bad.

He parked next to the curb. Clara's car was in

her driveway so he assumed she hadn't left for Spokane like Katelyn had suggested. He prayed just this once that Clara wouldn't look out her window and see him. Even if she did, he hoped she kept to herself. He was in no mood to have a friendly conversation or be patient. Besides, anyone who got near him was either in danger or ended up dead.

That's why he'd had to leave Katelyn behind.

The wind picked up. Clouds built in the distance, easily seen when lightning brightened inside them. What was with this sudden onslaught of storms in a usually dry climate? The thoughts morphed into much darker questions.

Would Mia still be alive if he hadn't pressured her to tell him the truth? If he hadn't been so suspicious? Was the domino effect Hunley had mentioned truly due to Beck's continued search and ultimate discovery of the safe?

Thunder rumbled, the sound getting louder as the storms moved closer.

As he walked through the rubble and stood in the middle of the burned-out home, he kicked a few pieces of unrecognizable lumps he guessed used to be furniture, and let dry sobs build in his chest. He should let the tears fall if they came. No one could see him except God, who saw everything, even the hidden tears in his heart.

"What should I do?" he whispered.

Did he actually believe he could make it to Langley? And with incriminating evidence and a CIA operative on his heels? Unfortunately, he didn't. But how did he get the truth into the right person's hands, if Mia and Barr had both been killed over this? How was Beck, with no real operative training, to survive when they couldn't?

That was it then, he would need to go undercover and on the run—with his family—while he made his way to hand over the information.

He would go as Travis Hinckley, the ID that Mia had supplied.

I'm sorry, Katelyn. He thought she might have held an ounce of hope that he would come back to town and all would be well. They could be "friends."

Beck hung his head. He plodded over to Ollie's room. How did he tell his son about his room? Ollie wasn't so shallow that his material things would matter that much to him, but still, he was just a kid. This would be so hard.

Then he spotted a Pokémon tin. Really? That had survived? He smiled. He had at least one item he could return to his son… It was something.

His cell rang with a number he didn't recognize. Sweat bloomed on his palms—instinctively he knew this call wasn't a wrong number. Dread coiled around his spine.

"Beck speaking."

"You have something I want."

"Who is this?"

"You know who it is."

Cooley. "I'm afraid I don't. I'm going to hang up—"

"Not if you want to see your son again."

TWENTY

All the blood drained out of him and his heart stopped. Had he understood the man correctly? Was Beck's unimaginable nightmare happening? He squeezed the phone in his hands, might have been crushing it, but he caught himself.

"What do you want?"

"You know what I want. But so there won't be any mistake, everything that was in the safe you took."

"Look, I don't have everything. Some junk I threw away. So tell me what you're really after."

A few heartbeats thumped by and for a moment, Beck thought he'd lost the signal. But he wouldn't be the first to speak. Somehow, for Ollie's sake, he had to get the upper hand.

Right. The guy had him, and he knew it.

Beck wanted to ask about his parents, too. He hadn't heard from them, so they could be bound or…

No. He wouldn't think the worst about them.

He would crumple if he did and he had to be strong for Ollie.

"Bring what you have. If what I'm looking for isn't there, you can say goodbye to your son."

"How do I know Ollie is with you?"

He heard a shuffling, then… "Dad?" Fear quaked in Ollie's voice.

"Ollie!"

"Now you know."

"Don't hurt him, do you hear me? Don't hurt him or I'll—"

"Or you'll what?"

"I'll hunt you down and make you wish you were dead."

Silence was all he heard in response. His hands sweated profusely until he thought he would drop the phone. He swiped each palm on his pants, as he stood in the middle of his razed home, the scent of wet ash filling his nostrils. Eyes squeezed shut, he pressed the cell against his ears and fisted his free hand.

Hold it together. For Ollie, just hold it together.

"Tell me where you want to meet so I can get my son back. I don't care about anything else. You can have it all." *I just want Ollie back safe and sound. I'm so sorry, son. So, so sorry.* If only he had left well enough alone!

"If you tell anyone—call the police or share

with your girlfriend at any point now or later—your son's life will be snatched from him. You know we can do this. You've seen it with your own eyes."

Mia...

"Do you understand?"

"Yes."

"I hear in your voice that you do, in fact, understand. You saw how quickly your wife died when she tried to share what she knew. Remember her."

"I understand." He fisted his free hand, imagining that hand around this man's throat and squeezing, squeezing, squeezing. He could hardly bark out the next question. "Where do we meet?"

"The place you know best."

Beck scratched his head. "My house is gone."

"Your work."

"What? You mean—"

"Castle Crags. Head that way. I'll call you with more information in half an hour. I can see a long distance from where I'm standing. Don't believe you can bring anyone with you. Come alone."

The call ended.

Beck fought the anguish, the mad rushing tears. Once again he resisted crushing the phone he held in his hand. His knees buckled, and he dropped.

"I'm here with you, Beck. I'm going with you." Katelyn.

A fist squeezed Katelyn's heart. Seeing him like this crushed her. She rushed to where he'd dropped to his knees in the ashes of his burned home.

He looked up at her and she saw the shimmering moisture in his eyes.

Oh, Beck. She couldn't bear seeing him like this. This ordeal had broken this strong resilient man into a thousand pieces. And yet, she knew he wouldn't break under this pressure, but would only be made stronger. He would pull himself together for his son's sake. If Katelyn knew anything, she knew that about this man.

"What. Are. You. Doing here?" He scrambled to his feet. Gripped her shoulders and shook her. "What are you doing? I don't want to have to worry about you, too."

"Okay. You're angry. I get that. But you have to worry about Ollie. Friends don't leave friends."

"Did you come to your house and spot me here? Did Clara see me and call you?"

"Nothing so covert. I—I thought you might

come here first, looking for answers. Or to say goodbye."

His expression softened. "You know me that well? I didn't even know I was coming here."

She gave a one-shoulder shrug. "I wasn't sure I'd find you here. But I did, and I overheard your conversation. At least your side of it and it's enough for me to know that he took Ollie. Cooley took Ollie. It has to be him. He's the one who took out Hunley and the other assassin."

"I'm supposed to come alone."

"As far as he knows, you will be. I'll be in the truck with you. I'll hide. Now let's not waste time arguing about it. I can make my own choices, Beck. I know where you're going. I overheard that part, too."

"If I bring someone I could risk Ollie's life, Katelyn!"

She grabbed his hands and spoke gently, hoping he would listen to reason. "If you go alone you risk both your lives."

Beck dipped his chin, contemplated for several moments, and then finally said, "Let's go then."

They rushed to his truck and got in. He started the ignition and raced down the street. "So you have to tell me just how did you get away from your family? I thought you'd never escape your three law-enforcement brothers."

No doubt about it—her brothers would be furious. Tori would be worried. But they wouldn't find out until it was too late.

"I wasn't a prisoner, Beck."

"So you snuck out like a teenager."

"Nope. Instead of a bachelor or bachelorette party, Tori and Ryan were attending a small party given by close friends. I was invited, but they knew I was exhausted and heartbroken." She couldn't help the grin. "I stayed behind when they left, and then I simply slipped away. I'll text Tori later that I went home to go to bed. She'll understand."

He shook his head. "I don't get you. I gave you an out. I don't understand why you came back."

"I told you. Friends don't leave friends." And with the words, she knew what she'd tried to ignore since getting into this. What she felt for Beck was so much more than platonic.

None of that mattered when Ollie's life was in danger.

"What about your parents?" Katelyn asked.

"I didn't ask about them. I was afraid to bring them up. But I should call them now. It's just that… I don't think I'm going to get an answer." He steered with one hand and tugged his cell out of his pocket with the other. Made the call. The longer he went without getting an answer, the deeper his frown grew. Finally, he said, "It's Beck. Call me immediately."

He focused on the road and glanced at his cell. "Calling Mom this time."

Again, he waited, then, "Mom, this is Beck. Please call me as soon as you get this message."

He ended the call and gripped the steering wheel with both hands. He didn't have to say anything for Katelyn to know he was in anguish.

"I'm so sorry."

"I can only worry about one person at a time."

She understood. He worried about his parents but his focus was on Ollie. "You don't need to worry about me or expend energy. I'm here to help. I'm not your hired PI, but I am a former cop. I'll help you get Ollie back."

He was taking the corners at crazy speeds.

"You should watch out so you don't get pulled over and delayed."

"Right. You're right." He slowed down the vehicle. "So let's think about this. He's going to call me and redirect. We can't know where the end will be. Somehow you need to slip out without him knowing and get into position so you can grab Ollie."

"Let's agree on something up front," she said. "And that is that you're not going to do anything stupid and get yourself killed."

"I wouldn't dream of it. And what I want to agree on up front is your one job is to grab Ollie. Nothing else matters. That's your only task. I'll distract Cooley with the contents of the safe, and you protect my son. I'm trusting you to do this one thing, so I'm begging you."

He was asking her to do the one thing she'd failed at before—save someone being used as a hostage.

TWENTY-ONE

Beck tried to focus as he drove toward Castle Crags, but all he could think about was poor Ollie. His little boy hadn't asked for any of this. Didn't deserve it—as if anyone deserved this to happen. But Ollie deserved better than this. Beck owed his little boy safety and security. That he and Mia had had lived their lives in an illusion for almost the entire time they were married shattered Beck.

Oh, Mia...

Why did she have to fall in love with Beck? Why couldn't she gain her freedom? Beck wished he had never searched for that safe and didn't know that Mia had left incriminating secrets against her old boss. Now the man would kill Beck and his son. He harbored no hope that he—or Katelyn—would be kept alive if Cooley somehow got the upper hand.

So together, they had to make their way out of this. Their release would not depend on Cooley, especially after what he'd done to Mia. There was no way the man could be trusted.

Beck hadn't had time to argue with Katelyn about coming with him, but she was fully aware that she could be sacrificing her own life now. She was going to help him get Ollie back.

She was right. She'd been right all along. He needed her. But so help him, he hadn't wanted to need her.

She'd said she'd come to him as a friend. *Friends don't leave friends*... But what he felt for her went beyond friendship, and she knew that.

But they had both drawn their own invisible lines they each refused to cross—both of them suffering with severe trust issues. Even though they danced around those lines, he knew that when this was over, if they survived, he would have to break both their hearts.

Best not to think about any of it considering they might not survive this. Beck forced his focus back to the curvy mountain roads as he steered through the Castle Crags Wilderness in Shasta-Trinity National Forest on his approach.

"Don't forget, I need to get out of this vehicle while I have the chance," she said.

"I can't risk him calling and directing me somewhere else, and then what? Just crunch down in the seat."

"If he has any kind of special vision detector, like night-vision goggles or heat-sensing equipment, he might see my heat signature. What about Ollie, Beck? Just let me get out right now and right here. It can't be much farther, can it? Worst case is you can come back and pick me up."

Ollie was already dead whether or not Katelyn had come, and in fact, she was their only hope. He didn't want to tell her that he was thinking that way. He didn't want to put that burden on her. Slowing the vehicle, he glanced at his watch. The call should have come through fifteen minutes ago.

He looked at his cell. He had a signal, though only a bar.

Katelyn had climbed into the back seat and scrunched onto the floorboard to hide.

He pounded the steering wheel and stopped.

"What's going on?" she whispered.

"I don't know. He was supposed to call me in half an hour."

"Maybe that had been a simple generalization."

"Maybe. Okay. Maybe." He started forward again. *Come on, and call. Call me!*

"What if you just call him back? His number is on your phone, isn't it?"

"Maybe he wants me to sweat. To be worried

about my son, and I am worried." Fear curdled in his gut.

He continued urging the truck slowly forward, watching the woods around them. They'd escaped the approaching storm but it would soon catch up to them. The sun had already dropped behind the mountains and dusk would create deep shadows in this forest much too soon. He still didn't have his Ollie back yet. *God, please let Ollie be all right. Please... Just let him get away.*

Beck thought about Ollie's smile that looked so much like Mia's. His giggle and wit and amazing sense of humor. No father could ask for a better son. Beck had spent all his spare time with Ollie and he had even taught him to climb here at Castle Crags. Mia had joined in on that family activity.

His breath hitched. Ollie had climbed the mountains with him here. Ollie both knew his way around this forest and how to climb those granite spirals—if he could just get away he could make it to safety all on his own. *God, please let him get away.* Ollie was smart. Still, the thought sent fear through him—Cooley could shoot him for his efforts.

Besides, his little boy was probably scared to death. Much too scared to act on his knowledge of this area, which was exactly how Beck was feeling at the moment. Paralysis was slowly taking hold of him, as if he'd ingested a paralytic poison. Cooley had mentioned the place that Beck knew well. Breath whooshed from him at the realization.

Cooley likely also knew that Ollie could climb.

Once again he glanced at his cell. "He called. He called and my phone didn't ring."

Beck slammed on the brakes and put his vehicle in Park. He returned the call. It went to voice mail. He ended the call, fearing he would say the wrong thing. "No, no, no! I didn't hear the cell, you idiot."

He recalled the number at the same time his cell indicated he had an incoming call.

"Relax, Beck. Slow and easy," he said, coaching himself.

He took a slow calming breath and tried to make his big, clumsy shaking fingers receive the call, and answered, "Beck."

"I told you to come alone."

Katelyn remained frozen in place as she listened to the voice echoing over the cell phone through the cab of the vehicle.

Cooley knew she was here? Her gut clenched. Squeezing her eyes shut, she prayed for Ollie...

Oh, God, please, please, keep him safe.

"You want the evidence, then give me my boy." Beck's tone was forceful. Threatening.

Through all of this, she had never heard or seen this side of him. He'd been crushed and the pieces of his soul thrown to the wind, but now it was as if the strong rock-climbing man she'd known—all of him had coalesced and was ready for this one moment. The energy built up inside the tiger who was ready to pounce and unleash his anger.

"I'll expect you to bring the private investigator with you to our meeting."

"No."

"No? What was your plan, Goodwin? To let her come up behind? You distract me and then she'll grab your son?"

"Nothing so elaborate."

"Remember, I call the shots for a living. Even your wife, another of my operatives, wasn't able to outmaneuver me."

Katelyn's heart pounded. How were they going to get out of this alive? She had to think of something, except Beck had given her one job. One task. And this time, she wouldn't—couldn't—fail, or Ollie would die.

"I'll remember," Beck said. "Now where are we meeting?"

"Keep driving another six hundred yards, then stop."

The line went dead and the vehicle started forward.

She hated asking him, but she couldn't read him so well right now. She wanted to make sure they were tracking the same. "What do you want me to do now, Beck?"

"You might as well get into the front seat. You were right—he was able to detect you were inside the truck. Your heat signature or something. Whatever. Somehow he knew."

Katelyn climbed into the front seat as he suggested. "I'm sorry. I didn't mean to complicate things. I only wanted to help. And I will help, if you'll just tell me what you're planning."

"You've put yourself at risk, Katelyn. I'm the one who is sorry. I shouldn't have let you do it. I tried to stop you. I think… I think there's still a chance that you can help save Ollie."

Beck slowed as he approached the six-hundred-yard point. "I didn't want to tell you this before. To put this pressure on you, but I think you just might be the only hope Ollie has."

Beck suddenly stopped, then turned. Cupped her cheeks and pulled her to him. He gave her a long, thorough kiss. Raw and desperate. She felt the rush of fear and emotion swirling out of him and rushing into her. Her heart quivered— she was anxious about what was to come. Torn about what she could lose if he was putting it all on her. He kissed her as if it was goodbye. As if he would never kiss her, or anyone, again. He'd never get the chance.

Oh, Lord... When I walk through the water... I'm about to get overwhelmed here. Help me!

Beck released her, then started the vehicle moving forward again. She understood they didn't have time to work out their lives when Ollie's was on the line.

"Understand me, Katelyn. I'm going to cause a distraction. I don't know what or how, but you'll know when you see it. Your job, your *only* job, is to get him to safety. Don't worry about me. I can take care of myself. Ollie is depending on us both. Do you understand?"

"Beck, I—"

"Do. You. Understand?"

"Yes…" She choked out the word. "You're going to give your life for his."

"If it comes to that, then yes, of course. If my life will give him a chance to live, then I'm expendable."

TWENTY-TWO

Beck parked his vehicle in the middle of the forest road. Heart pounding, he opened the door a crack. "This is it."

Thunder sounded. The storm would be on top of them soon. Trees rustled as the wind whipped.

Ollie would be so scared. He'd always been scared of the lightning. Mia would sometimes hold him at night during a rare thunderstorm until it passed or he fell asleep.

Beck wasn't sure if he should wait in the truck for another phone call or not, but he would get out and see what happened. He hopped from the vehicle, then slammed the door to announce his arrival.

Katelyn shut her door and walked to the front of the vehicle, where Beck joined her.

"Okay. I'm here," he shouted. "I want my son."

Standing in the middle of the road lined with evergreen forest on each side, Beck realized this was a setup for an ambush if he'd ever seen one.

"Daddy?" Ollie's shaky voice sounded small.

"Ollie! Ollie, where are you?" Beck whirled and let his eyes search the darkening forest.

Katelyn tugged on his arm. He followed where she pointed.

Cooley stepped onto the road about fifteen feet in front of them.

"Daddy?" Ollie tried to run but Cooley gripped the back of his jacket. He lifted his gun and pointed it at Ollie's temple.

Grief exploded inside Beck. He kept his chin up. His act together. His son needed to see that his father was confident that he would free them both. Beck hoped his demeanor and false confidence would replace the dread curdling in his gut.

"Let him go, Cooley." Beck hoped he sounded more forceful than he felt.

"Did you bring it?" The man growled the question.

"Beck, he could kill us all and take it from the vehicle." Katelyn ground out the words in a low tone.

Beck offered a subtle nod, letting her know that he understood.

The man yanked Ollie so that he cried out.

"How do I know you won't just kill us once you have what you want?"

"You don't." The man laughed.

Of all the… Beck would play a game of his own. It was all he had. "That's why I only brought most of it."

"You'd risk your son's life?"

"Absolutely not. You don't hand him over now, you won't see anything."

He heard the barely audible intake of breath from Katelyn. He could imagine her question.

What are you doing?

Beck had to overcome this mountain. He had to master it. To climb it. He saw Cooley as a potentially deadly spike of granite and Beck. Would. Master. Him. He would keep telling himself the same words he used when tackling a new climb. Let Cooley see in Beck a man not to be trifled with.

He tried to remain calm, but his heart pounded as he waited a few breaths for Cooley to respond.

"All right," Cooley said. "Bring it forward. Then you can find out if I like what I see."

"Katelyn…get the box."

In his peripheral vision, he saw her jerk her head to him.

"Just…get the Pokémon box."

Katelyn returned and handed over the tin box. Her eyes drilled into him but she said nothing. She knew like he knew that it only contained

Pokémon cards. Ridiculous they survived the fire. She also knew what he required of her.

She subtly shook her head.

"You're wasting time," Cooley said. "You have ten seconds to walk this way and hand over the goods or I'm going to shoot him execution-style."

Cooley shoved Ollie to the ground. "On your knees." He pointed the weapon at the back of Ollie's head.

Katelyn gasped next to him. Beck's heart almost stopped and he stumbled as he walked forward, showing his weakness and fear.

To his credit, Ollie said nothing. He didn't cry out. This experience would change him forever, and Beck felt the strength he somehow gathered in these last few moments quickly fading.

Was he doing the right thing? Was he risking Ollie's life?

After all, what did he care if Cooley had the information? Except, they would all be killed if he gave over his last bargaining chip, so he hadn't even brought it. He'd buried it beneath the ash of what remained of the house he'd shared with Mia and Ollie.

Stunned, Katelyn forced her shaking legs to walk alongside Beck. Wind gusted and blew her hair into her face and she shoved it away.

Beck had not brought the items that would save his son's life. She still couldn't grasp that move on his part.

But Beck was thinking far ahead—Cooley wouldn't allow them to live. Beck knew this was his last and only chance to save his son. And then to keep them safe in the future, he would deliver the information to some higher-up at Langley. Somehow. Some way.

But to have the confidence, the nerve, to go through with it blew her away. She was trained law enforcement but Beck was showing his true grit by standing up to this guy. Beck was a rock. A master at tackling challenges, and she hadn't seen that coming.

Nor had she expected the rest to unfold the way it had.

She tried to remain completely aware of her surroundings and stay alert and ready for the "distraction" Beck had mentioned. She suspected he didn't know what it was yet, so couldn't tell her, but he would know when to act. She had to be ready.

She could do this. She could save Ollie. *Oh, Lord, please save us all!*

She had to remain strong through this. Katelyn thought back to all her police-academy and on-the-job training, but nothing in real life ever went according to the training.

When Tony had been overcome by a criminal with a gun, the unexpected had happened. Katelyn had to be prepared for the unexpected right now.

How did one prepare for the unknown?

Still on his knees, Ollie lifted his head to stare at his father. Hope and fear warred in his gaze. His eyes soon dropped to what Beck carried.

"What's in the Pokémon box, Dad?"

Oh, no. Ollie spotted his Pokémon box. Surely he didn't care if the cards were traded for his life.

"Ollie, it's going to be okay."

"I want to know what you're giving him in exchange for me? What's so important? Is it money? Am I being ransomed?"

"Your mom left some things behind. I found them in a safe. They're secret things that this man wants. He used to work with her, and he is forcing me to give them to him."

"Not Mom's stuff!" Ollie was in a full-on panic now. Tears and anger spilled from him.

"Relax, son."

Cooley yanked on his hair and pressed the gun barrel into his temple, deeper, harder. This time Ollie cried out.

"Stop it!" Katelyn yelled. "How dare you terrify a little boy."

"You can stop right there." Cooley gestured at the ground with the gun. "Set the box down. Then back away. I'll come forward and look. I'll decide if you deserve to live."

"I brought what you asked. Keep your end of the deal."

"You said you only brought part of it, and I can appreciate you're trying to use it for leverage. I'll give you that."

"How generous."

Katelyn tried to get Ollie's attention and hold his eyes. She hoped he could read in hers that he should run to her. They should run together when Beck distracted Cooley.

When was that going to happen?

They were running out of time. It would have to be soon. She tried to think ahead. When Cooley bent over for the box, that moment when his gun wasn't trained on Ollie—in that one single split moment in time, Beck would have to draw Cooley's attention.

Katelyn would have to save Ollie.

Her pulse raged in her ears as the storm increased. The wind picked up and a few big drops of rain hit her in the face.

Beck set the Pokémon tin on the ground and stepped back.

"Keep going until I say stop."

"No. You bring Ollie forward. You get the box when I get Ollie."

"I could just shoot you here and take it."

"And risk not getting everything you wanted? I don't think so."

Oh, Beck. Katelyn had no idea from what pocket Beck pulled his boldness.

"No. You can't take Mom's stuff." Ollie suddenly burst away from Cooley, dashed forward and dove for the box.

Cooley aimed to shoot him. Ollie rolled away.

"No!" Beck rammed into Cooley, throwing his aim off.

Katelyn grabbed for Ollie, but he took the box and sprinted into the woods.

TWENTY-THREE

Thunder boomed through his chest, followed by a crack as lightning hit a nearby tree and split it open. Half the trunk plunged toward them. Cooley straddled Beck with his fist ready to strike Beck's face, but rolled away as the tree hurtled toward them.

Beck scrambled up and out of harm's way just in time. The trunk thudded against the ground, wood chips splintering and flying as the trunk bounced. Beck gave the tree a wide berth and caught a glimpse of Cooley sprinting into the woods.

"Ollie!" Beck shouted. "Ollie, run. Get far away. You know your way around. You can do this!"

The man was going after Ollie and the Poké-mon box. Beck raced after Cooley and entered the woods that grew darker by the minute. The storm winds picked up and the evergreens rustled with the wind, sounding like a thousand whispers.

Lightning flashed again and again, coupled with thunder claps.

Would any of them survive this?

"Ollie!" Beck called out to his son, but if Ollie answered, then Cooley could find him, too.

"Ollie, run. Get away. Cooley's coming."

In reality he'd been running around in the dark for five minutes, but it felt like hours. He paused next to a tree to catch his breath. Where would Ollie go? He was scared but smart. Strong like his dad. He'd done his best to instill confidence in the boy and this was the time he needed to rely on that. Then he thought he knew where Ollie would go.

Lightning flashed and he spotted Cooley's silhouette in the distance. The man had retrieved his gun and held it at the ready.

Good. Cooley was heading in the wrong direction. Beck kept going, jogging as fast as he could, though the underbrush was thick in places. His heart pounded but he kept going and wouldn't stop until he found Ollie. Beck climbed over the boulders at the base of the crags where Ollie could hide and dashed around them, searching for his son.

Beck hoped he was the only one struggling to find a way out of this, and that Ollie was well on his way to safety. At the same time, he wanted to find his son. Needed to know he was safe. He thought he knew where Ollie would go, but so far he hadn't found him. *Where are you, Ollie?*

He was thinking about this all wrong.

Ollie wouldn't simply hide, he would try to climb to escape.

Beck's heart hammered at the thought.

Beck changed course and headed for Vista Point Trail, running through cedars and dogwoods. If he was Ollie, that's what he would have done, and his kid was enough like him to think the same way. But nothing in life had prepared either of them to face off with this sort of evil. Beck ran toward the base of the jagged granite spirals, the place he'd taken Ollie in the past to start their climb. Only they had protective gear and ropes. This—this was dangerous, and part of him hoped that Ollie had gone a different way.

Part of him hoped Ollie wouldn't try to free climb. One mistake could kill.

Finally, he reached the heart of the Crags. He glanced up. Castle Dome stood tall and lofty like a sentinel over the region.

Ollie…

He worried about Katelyn but trusted she was out there searching for Ollie, too. He hoped she'd already found him and secured his safety.

That he'd grabbed the box and taken off like that had surprised them all, and served as the distraction that Beck had needed. Up to that point, he had been flailing to find a way to distract Cooley without causing more harm to Ollie.

Ollie had been the one to give them a chance.

Beck was sure God had something to do with it, too. He always did.

Don't worry, Ollie, Katelyn. I'm coming.

Beck weaved up the steep wall of the dome's first section, then paused to look around.

No Ollie.

Bending over his thighs, he caught his breath. "Ollie… Where…are you?"

"Here, Dad. I'm here." The voice was small.

He whirled and spotted his son huddled in a space between two boulders. Shivering, Ollie held out the opened Pokémon box, Pokémon cards spilling out. Tears rushed down his cheeks.

Beck ran forward and drew him into his arms. "Oh, Ollie. I'm so proud of you. You got away. You got to safety."

He released Ollie and crouched at eye level. "Are you okay?"

Ollie's eyes remained huge. "I think so. Mimi and Pops will be worried, though."

Beck tensed. He hadn't wanted to ask about them yet. "You mean Cooley didn't harm them?"

Ollie shook his head. "Pops got sick so we had to go home. Mimi was taking care of him. I went outside—Pikachu was missing." Mimi's cat. "And then, he took me. He let Pikachu get away, but he took me."

Mom and Dad would have tried to call Beck. So what Ollie said didn't make sense. They could be tied up somewhere. He had to focus on getting Ollie to safety, but he could call the police and get someone to his parents' home. He held up his cell. No signal.

"Dad, I thought the box held some of Mom's things."

Beck ruffled Ollie's hair. "I'll explain everything, I promise, but right now Cooley wants to kill us. He wants to kill Katelyn, too. We have to get somewhere safe. You understand, don't you?"

The anger and confusion in Ollie's eyes seemed to clear as he nodded. "Okay. I came here to climb and get away. I thought… I thought I could climb, but I don't have the ropes. I didn't have you. I can't go without you."

"But you did the right thing. I suspected you would come here, and I came to find you. Cooley is out there in those woods with a gun. If we can make it up to our spot we'll be safe from him. We've done this a hundred times, Ollie." And Beck could possibly get that signal.

Ollie nodded. "I'll leave the box here. I don't think Cooley wanted the cards. We'll come back for it, won't we?"

"Yes, we will."

Beck grabbed Ollie's hand and together they headed up the dome—where Beck had trained for free climbing many times. "You got this," he said.

They followed the quartz vein along the granite toward the porch on the dome's east side. There the ground would drop away, down sheer cliffs. After the porch came the gully, and then the final pitch, which was a class four. They'd need rope for that.

"We're stopping here, Ollie."

"I know. We need rope. You haven't taken me yet."

"Maybe one day."

They found a place to rest, where they often would come to look at the view.

Father and son. And talk about the deeper things of life. Here all was quiet and the world was right again. Here Beck could be closer to God, and to his son.

Here Cooley couldn't get to them.

Beck wished Katelyn was with them, and guilt warred inside that he was here with Ollie but had left her to fend for herself. But she'd reminded him a hundred times she was an ex-cop. One had to pick and choose their battles, and right now, Beck wanted to get Ollie away from the madman who had killed Beck's wife, and was gunning to kill them all.

He tugged out his cell phone to call 911 and then Katelyn.

A big drop hit Beck in the face. Then another. Then the storm clouds released a downpour.

"Dad!" Ollie slipped.

Rain hammered the forest. Though the trees shielded her from the brunt of it, Katelyn was hit with a few pine needles, along with water drops, as rivulets washed debris away in places. Splashing through them, she searched for Ollie.

That had been her only job, the most important job she would ever have—to keep that little boy safe.

That a bullet had grazed Katelyn shouldn't have stopped her. That wound bled profusely now because her heart pounded and adrenaline surged. Gasping for breath, she leaned against a tree, ripped the sleeve from her soaked blouse and wrapped her arm. At least the rain had washed the wound a bit. She should have done that to begin with, but she thought she could catch up with the boy. He had somehow disappeared—and not just him.

She'd heard Beck shouting for Ollie, but she

hadn't seen him. She'd been beyond relieved to hear his voice because she'd left him fighting with Cooley. She had no doubt that Beck could get the best of Cooley, the coward.

She'd heard Beck shout that Cooley was coming. So he was out here, too.

The cold wind and rain whipped around her. She couldn't remember the last time it had stormed like this.

Ollie had made a run for it more than twenty minutes ago, she guessed. Good for him. Good for him that he got away and gave them a distraction, but now what? She wiped the rain from her eyes and face, then pushed from the tree trunk, ready to search again.

She remained wary of Cooley, who would still be out here searching, too. He wanted that box. And he wanted them dead. They were the only witnesses. She wished he would leave. Clearly he hadn't won this battle, which only meant he would come for them again when they least expected it.

No. That couldn't happen. They had to get him today. Take him down today.

The rain slowed to a steady beat instead of a tumultuous hammering downpour. Katelyn ignored her shivering and tried to hold her weapon steady. The forest was dark in the shadow of the crags. Lightning flashed in the distance as the storm moved on. She strained to see well and needed to pull out her flashlight, but feared that would definitely give her away to Cooley.

A branch caught her foot and she stumbled forward and fell into the wet pine needles face-first. Her gun slid across the needles beneath a fallen, rotting tree trunk

With the rain trickling through the trees and the rumbling thunder in the distance, she struggled to hear any sounds that would warn of approaching danger.

She scrambled to her feet.

Cooley stood near and held a gun. He'd seen her too. She dove behind a tree as gunfire ricocheted through the forest. Katelyn gasped for breath. Her weapon was somewhere beneath that fallen trunk. Somehow she had to make her way around to get the gun.

Forget her burning arm.

She was moments away from certain death.

Remaining frozen in place behind the tree, she calmed her breathing and listened. The forest was eerie with shadows cast when lightning flashed and raindrops pattering through the trees and plopping on the needle-laden ground, muting the sound.

She detected the slightest motion.

And held her breath.

Cooley... He was near. He had to be near.

What am I going to do?

Her only choice was to make a dash for her gun and hope he wasn't quick enough to shoot her in the back.

That didn't seem like much of a choice. She needed another choice.

Holding her breath, Katelyn remained as quiet as possible and hoped he wouldn't find her. Heart pounding, her pulse roared in her ears.

Then Cooley stepped directly in front of her, the muzzle of his gun pointed in her face.

Oh, God, help me...

He lifted the weapon and swung the grip toward her head.

TWENTY-FOUR

"You're doing great, Ollie."

At least up on the crags, darkness hadn't yet descended. They had barely enough light and needed to get down while they still could. As they made their way down the Castle Dome, the rocks were slippery, but Beck and Ollie had trained on this climb before and knew every place to step. He wanted to stay so that Ollie would be safe, but with the wind so harsh, Ollie had slipped. Beck had caught him. But the crags weren't safe, either, after all, so they made their way down. Beck had thought this was the best way to escape Cooley. At the top, Beck had called 911 and explained their emergency as succinctly as he could.

A man with a gun with intent to harm was on the trails.

He didn't go into the fact the man was a CIA operative or supervisor—that would make it sound like a crank call. Katelyn's brothers could hear the news on the police radio and come for them.

Then he'd texted Katelyn. He needed to know if she was okay. He waited for her reply for a few minutes. She could be hiding or in a bad situation. Or she could simply be searching and lost.

He'd heard gunfire and his gut clenched.

He'd left Katelyn to fend for herself. Guilt suffused him. How did he keep Ollie safe and help Katelyn? Sure, she'd been a former cop, but cops depended on backup.

Friends never leave friends...

His only thought for his son, he'd left Katelyn behind, trusting that she would be okay.

Had the gunfire been from her gun? Or Cooley's?

He led the way down, and if Ollie slipped again, he would once again reinforce his moves. Reposition him if necessary. Granite could be climbed wet or dry, so the rain didn't hinder them too much.

"Only a little more, Ollie. You've got this."

Finally Beck hopped down and reached up to grab his boy from the rocks. He held him long and hard. "Ollie, I need to find Katelyn. I'm worried about her. But I don't want to take you into danger."

"You want me to hide, don't you?"

He released Ollie and gripped his arms. "Hide and wait for me."

Tears streamed from Ollie's face. "I can't, Dad. Take me with you. That's the safest place for me."

Beck thought he'd never heard wiser words. "You know something, you're right."

He tugged his son to him, hoping for life to return to normal. He hadn't even told Ollie about the house. Considering how he acted over the box he thought contained his mother's things, news of the house fire would be devastating.

But first things first. They weren't out of this yet.

Beck took a long breath. "We just have to take the trail down now."

They continued along the trail that led out of the area at the base of the crags and drew near the woods.

Beck stopped and eyed the forest.

"What are we doing, Dad?"

Ollie's eyes were big and round and blue, and Beck saw Mia there, in his son. How did he make him understand? How did he keep his boy safe and also save the girl?

Ollie's eyes widened. "Dad!"

Beck whirled around, keeping his body in front of his son. Cooley stood ten yards away, aiming his weapon at them.

"I should kill you now. Blow both your heads off. But I need the box."

"Where's Katelyn?" Beck asked.

"No need to worry about her. I took care of her. You're a failure, Beck. Mia should never have married you. I warned her that she wouldn't be happy settling down, especially with the likes of you. A big dumb athlete."

Beck tried not to let the words cut him, eat away at him. Mia was gone. What did the words matter? But his heart bled, the wound opening back up. And now to hear that he'd let down Katelyn, that she was dead too... Beck's knees almost buckled.

He still had this one last chance. This last chance to save his son. Ollie had to live, no matter the cost.

"What have you done with it, boy?"

"I'll never tell you!" Ollie shouted.

Cooley fired his gun into the ground near Beck's feet. He almost flinched but maintained his composure. "Ollie lost the box. He doesn't know where he left it. You're free to search."

"That's a lie. He wanted his mother's things bad enough to risk everything."

Well, Cooley had been paying attention and that didn't help them right now.

"Boy, the next shot is going into your father's gut. Did you know that's one of the most painful ways to die? You bleed out slowly. It can take—"

"Stop it!" Beck took a step forward.

Cooley lifted his weapon higher, aiming more toward Beck's chest. "You see, if he dies slowly, you'll have time to say goodbye to dear old dad. Otherwise, I could just shoot him in the heart and he dies instantly. Or a bullet to the head."

"Dad." Ollie choked out the word through tears. "I'm scared."

Beck reached over and squeezed Ollie's hand, reassuring him. He had no idea how he was going to get them out of this. If he could draw Cooley in a little closer, then he could ram him and Ollie could once again run. This time he could run to find a ranger station. But he could keep running until he was somewhere safe and never look back.

"I'll give you everything you want. I'll take you to the box right now, only let Ollie go. Let him live his life."

"Deal. You give me everything I asked for, then only one of you has to die *today*."

Beck didn't think he misinterpreted the hidden threat. He would die today, but Ollie didn't have much time to live.

Her vision blurry, she saw two of everything. Cooley had slammed her with the butt of his gun. That much she knew because she felt it with every single beat of her heart thundering through her head. All she could think was that he was done wasting bullets trying to kill her. Maybe his last two bullets were meant for Ollie and Beck. Cooley might have finished the job, though, if he'd been able to find *her* gun.

She had to get to Cooley before he used the last of his ammunition to kill two people she cared deeply about.

The voices had sounded through the trees and stirred her. Motivated her to get up and save Beck and Ollie. So she'd scrambled to her feet and found her gun, despite her throbbing head and double vision. Aching back and burning arm. That would all heal. But lives could not be recovered.

She could do this. She had to save them. This was the moment she could make it all right. She'd never wanted this moment or asked for it, but it was here. Katelyn had to help them.

Using the trees for support, she moved from one to the next until she finally got her balance and her double vision eased up.

The voices echoed against the crags leading her to them. Katelyn held her weapon high. She knew exactly what she had to do. But what she didn't know was if this was like the scene from *True Grit*, where the ranger helped save the others but was mortally wounded and died in the effort.

She couldn't think about that.

Beck and Ollie had to live even if she died.

As she crept forward, she finally saw the two men she had to save and blurred images of Cooley's back.

Katelyn crept quietly. Cooley was too busy making threats, and she was about to run out of time.

She wouldn't let them down.

But how did she shoot if her aim was definitely going to be off? She couldn't see straight.

God, help me take the shot. Help me make it right. I have no other choice. When I walk through the water...

"Cooley!" she called. "You should have killed me when you had the chance!"

Cooley whirled around and fired his weapon at the same moment Katelyn fired twice.

The man fell forward. Katelyn dropped to her knees. She could have missed and killed Beck or Ollie.

They ran toward her. Beck dropped next to her, and Ollie, too. The rock-climbing master held them both in his arms.

Beck gripped Katelyn to peer at her. "Are you okay?"

"He hit me in the head. I could have killed you just now. My vision is blurred. I feel sick."

"You've got a concussion. I called the police. Someone should be here." He glanced around. "But the woods are growing darker. I should get you out of here."

She rose. "Wait. We can't leave Cooley." Katelyn stumbled toward the man. If he wasn't dead, he was dying. "We should try to save him. Keep him alive until help can arrive. Call for an ambulance, too."

Cooley rolled to his side and aimed his gun at Katelyn.

"Katelyn!" Beck shouted.

She whirled as Beck rushed forward to block the shot, putting himself in harm's way and kicking the gun from Cooley's hand. Beck pressed his booted foot on the man's wrist. "Good news, Cooley, you're not going to die today. Not if we have anything to do with it."

A couple of rangers rushed forward from the woods. Deputies, too.

"We were responding to your emergency call near the crags," one ranger said, "and heard the gunfire."

Reece, Ben and Ryan emerged from the woods then too. Tori jogged right behind them.

Oh, great. Her whole family had come. Then again, what would she do without them? The rangers gave Cooley medical attention and called for a helicopter to lift him out and fly him to the nearest trauma center. Her family gathered around and hugged her.

"You need to see a doctor and fast. Maybe you should fly in the helicopter with Cooley," Ryan said.

"No. Just no, thank you."

"I'll take her." Beck stepped up, holding tight to Ollie.

"And your parents are okay, Beck. They were tied up and were able to free themselves. We received the emergency call from them moments ago."

Relief whooshed from Beck. "Thank you for letting me know."

Her brothers left her alone with Beck and Ollie while they spoke with the rangers. Detective Manning informed Cooley he was under arrest.

"There's still the matter of handing over this material to the right person," Beck said.

"You're afraid it's not over yet."

He nodded.

Beck's cell rang. An unknown number. Why was he getting a cell signal now, of all times? He held her gaze. "Here we go again."

"You should answer it, Beck. Let's get this

over with. No more hiding now. Everyone is going to know about this soon enough."

He put the phone on Speaker and answered. "Beck Goodwin."

"Mr. Goodwin. This is the Deputy Director of the CIA, Martin Kendall, speaking." Beck gave her an incredulous look.

She understood his shock. How did this guy know to call *him*?

She shrugged. He was the director of the CIA, after all. She was glad that he already knew enough to call Beck.

Katelyn smiled at Beck as they listened—it was over now. Truly over.

For the moment, she ignored the sudden fear that her time with Beck would be coming to an end. They would say their goodbyes and he would probably move away. Who would want to stay here near the Mount Shasta region after everything?

TWENTY-FIVE

Tori and Ryan's ceremony was as beautiful and special as any wedding could be. Katelyn fought the tears as she stood in her place as maid of honor next to the bride and watched her brother exchange vows with Tori. The Goodwin family had joined them today upon her invitation, and she kept wanting to glance out into the gathering at Beck.

Katelyn's mind kept going back to that moment when Beck had stepped in front of her to block Cooley's shot. He'd been ready to give his life for her, and in the end he'd saved her. He'd been ready to give his life for his son. A man like that could be trusted with her heart. She hadn't thought she could trust again, but there was nothing she wanted more than to give Beck her heart. But he'd struggled with trust himself after what he'd been through with his wife. So Katelyn should put aside her hopes.

Besides, this wasn't her day. This was Ryan and Tori's day.

Katelyn might not ever get a wedding day—she didn't think she would ever find another man like Beck.

After the pastor pronounced Tori and Ryan as man and wife and introduced Mr. and Mrs. Bradley to the crowd, Katelyn waited for her turn and then followed the wedding couple down the aisle and out into the foyer of the church. A reception was to follow in the fellowship hall.

Joy filled Katelyn's heart. *Thank You, God.* She'd made it through the ordeal of this week and Tori and Ryan had made it to the altar. Katelyn hugged and congratulated family members and swiped at the tears that kept escaping. Weddings always made her cry, and she wasn't sure why.

In her peripheral vision she spotted Beck standing back in the hallway with his family, as if preparing to leave. Katelyn excused herself and rushed to catch up with them. She tugged Beck's jacket and he turned.

Beck's eyes brimmed with admiration and so much more. "Katelyn, you look so beautiful." He leaned in and whispered, "More beautiful than the bride."

Then he stepped back and smiled. Her cheeks

warmed. "Thank you. Um… You're not leaving already, are you?"

"Mom and Dad are taking Ollie out. I was deliberating on what to do next. I wanted to at least say hi to you before I left, but…"

Beck had wanted her to believe in him and had often waited for her to say things. Well, this time, she wanted to hear him say it. She could invite him to stay, but she would hear it from him first.

"But?"

He studied her, searching her gaze, looking right through her soul like only he could. Had she truly only gotten to know this man so well in a week? Her throat grew tight and tears welled. The wedding stuff getting to her again.

Stepping closer, Beck pressed his hands against the bare skin of her arms. Fortunately the bullet-grazed part of her arm was partially covered. Considering the current that had always sparked between them, she wasn't sure she wanted him so close, touching her arms. A hum started in her belly.

"I wasn't sure if you wanted me to stay, Katelyn."

"Of course I want you to stay. You're all invited to the reception. But only if you want to be here, Beck. No pressure." Katelyn wanted to tell him more, but she needed to hear this from him.

"You believed me when no one else would," he said. "Not even my parents."

"I believed you."

"When I thought Cooley had taken you out, all I could think about was how I would give anything to have a chance with you. Because…"

He gently lifted her chin and leaned closer. "I'm free to trust now, Katelyn. All because of you. Free to trust, and free to love."

Again he searched her eyes and his gaze dropped to her lips. "What do you think about you and me? Is there a future for us?"

"I'm free to trust, too, Beck. I'm free to love." Exploring the possibility of love and a future with this man was all Katelyn wanted and joy filled her heart.

His lips found hers and slowly he wrapped his arms around her, drawing her closer, and kissed her with the promise of so much more.

When he ended the kiss, Katelyn found family members watching. Tori and Ryan clapped and the others joined in the applause. Katelyn's cheeks grew hot.

Tori tossed Katelyn her flowers, which, according to tradition, meant she would be the next among the bridesmaids to marry. She hoped Beck wasn't clued in to those traditions and flicked a glance at him.

"No pressure," he said and winked.

* * * * *

If you enjoyed this book, be sure to go back and pick up Tori and Ryan's story, Deadly Evidence.
And look for more books in Elizabeth Goddard's Mount Shasta Secrets miniseries!

Dear Reader,

Thank you for reading *Covert Cover-Up*. I hope you enjoyed reading it as much as I enjoyed writing it. I truly had so much fun writing this cloak-and-dagger tale. Setting always inspires me and I knew when I saw Castle Crags on our many drives through the region that I needed to set a story there. My Mount Shasta Secrets action-adventure romantic suspense series was born, and Beck was the perfect rock-climbing character for Castle Crags, wouldn't you agree? I have always loved the scripture found in Isaiah 43:2: "When thou passest through the waters, I will be with thee; and through the rivers, they shall not overflow thee: when thou walkest through the fire, thou shalt not be burned; neither shall the flame kindle upon thee." I thought this was the perfect scripture for Katelyn and what she was facing, because God is always with us as we walk through the troubles in this life.

I hope and pray that you'll trust that He's always with you no matter what. I hope you'll be sure to join me for the next book in the series—Reece Bradley's story. I love connecting with my readers. You can find out more about me at my website, ElizabethGoddard.com. You can also join me on Facebook, and I have a new private reader's group—contact me and ask me how you can join.

Blessings!
Elizabeth Goddard

Get 4 FREE REWARDS!

We'll send you 2 FREE Books plus 2 FREE Mystery Gifts.

Love Inspired books feature uplifting stories where faith helps guide you through life's challenges and discover the promise of a new beginning.

FREE Value Over $20

THE WESTERN HEARTS COLLECTION!

19 FREE BOOKS in all!

COWBOYS. RANCHERS. RODEO REBELS.

**Here are their charming love stories in one prized Collection:
51 emotional and heart-filled romances that capture the majesty
and rugged beauty of the American West!**

YES! Please send me **The Western Hearts Collection** in Larger Print. This collection begins with 3 FREE books and 2 FREE gifts in the first shipment. Along with my 3 free books, I'll also get the next 4 books from The Western Hearts Collection, in LARGER PRINT, which I may either return and owe nothing, or keep for the low price of $5.45 U.S./$6.23 CDN each plus $2.99 U.S./$7.49 CDN for shipping and handling per shipment*. If I decide to continue, about once a month for 8 months I will get 6 or 7 more books but will only need to pay for 4. That means 2 or 3 books in every shipment will be FREE! If I decide to keep the entire collection, I'll have paid for only 32 books because 19 books are FREE! I understand that accepting the 3 free books and gifts places me under no obligation to buy anything. I can always return a shipment and cancel at any time. My free books and gifts are mine to keep no matter what I decide.

☐ 270 HCN 5354   ☐ 470 HCN 5354

Name (please print)

Address   Apt. #

City   State/Province   Zip/Postal Code

Mail to the **Reader Service:**
IN U.S.A.: P.O. Box 1341, Buffalo, N.Y. 14240-8531
IN CANADA: P.O. Box 603, Fort Erie, Ontario L2A 5X3